OUT OF THE HODGEPODGE

PHYLLIS JAMISON

To my dear friends, Elaine & Frank Martin. With love, Phyllis Jamison

PublishAmerica
Baltimore

First printing

ISBN: 1-59286-426-0
PUBLISHED BY PUBLISHAMERICA, LLLP
www.publishamerica.com
Baltimore

Printed in the United States of America

With many thanks to supportive friends, members of Beaverton Senior Writers, and especially to my mentor, Sheila Stephens, for the guidance and encouragement that brought this project to fruition.

FOREWORD

Regardless of age, occupation, or status, most women's lives are a hodgepodge of responsibility and concern, with little opportunity, or even energy to escape. Frequently, however, short intervals of leisure do present themselves, and it is then that a craving occurs for some tidbit of literary art to refresh both mind and heart.

Out of the Hodgepodge is designed to do just that. Like the splash of a sparkling green fountain, like a whiff of cologne from a passing stranger, like a plump, ripe strawberry at the end of a heavy meal, short-short fiction can answer that craving. A book of such stories is like having at one's elbow a tray of assorted hors d'oeuvres. *Out of the Hodgepodge* is, itself, a hodgepodge of 50 stories, each a digestible 500 to 2000 words in length.

The inspirational source of these stories is a game I invented several years ago for my own amusement and to rescue myself from my own personal hodgepodge. By snatching words at random and using them in a single sentence, I have found a fountain from which all sorts of stories and characters have emerged. It has been great fun for me to produce them, and I hope you will find pleasure – and escape from your hodgepodge – in reading them.

– Phyllis Jamison

GRANDPA GUS
Based on Universal, Scraggly, Tease, Distraught

Gus Fergusson, Abernethy Park's universal grandpa, stroked his somewhat scraggly goatee with a wrinkled hand as he tried to tease a smile from Myra Moon, a young, unwed mother whom he knew to be distraught over unpaid bills and her baby's colic. Despite his unkempt appearance, Gus was known to be descended from the founding family of this small town. He was also known as its long-retired pharmacist, and a keen and kindly extra pair of eyes – and sometimes ears – among the bevy of mothers who brought their children to the park to play.

On this particular morning, Gus' attention was drawn to Myra, who had recently returned to her home town hoping for the support and comfort of family and lifelong friends, but who had received a chilly welcome. Upon hearing the mellow tones of the old man's voice, the baby paused in her crying and looked at him with tearful curiosity. This did, indeed, make Myra smile.

"You sure do have a way with babies," she said.

Gus sat down on the park bench next to her and the baby held out her arms to him.

"May I take her?" he asked.

"This is the first time she's stopped crying for hours," Myra said, gratefully relinquishing the child to him.

"Well, she's just glad to see Grandpa Gus. Aren't you, Toby," he said, cradling the wee girl in his arms.

Myra's face showed her relief, and an affectionate gaze replaced the misery and tension that had dwelt in her eyes only a few moments before. Toby grinned as she tugged at Gus' goatee, her distress apparently forgotten.

"How do you do that?" Myra asked.

"It's a secret," Gus told her. "A secret even from me." And he chuckled softly at his small joke.

Myra reached out to stroke Toby's fine brown hair and sighed, closing her eyes for a moment, and Gus took note of a blissful expression on her face.

"How long has it been since you've had any sleep?" he asked.

Myra opened her eyes and looked into his. "A while," she said. "I have a lot of worries, and poor Toby just cries so with her colic. I think my milk doesn't agree with her."

"Perhaps it's your worries that don't agree with her," Gus suggested gently.

Myra gave him a wry smile. "They don't do much for me, either."

"But you don't get to cry and have someone try to comfort you," Gus observed.

Myra was silent for a few moments, close to tears, acknowledging the truth of the old man's statement. "I do cry, sometimes," she said, then, "but it doesn't seem to help much."

"Do you have friends? A family?" Gus asked, knowing the truth, having heard the malicious gossip that had pervaded the town.

Myra shook her head sadly.

"How old are you?" he asked.

"Seventeen," she said, peering warily from behind the oily strands of hair that nearly obscured her face.

"Are you getting help from the State?"

Myra nodded. "I have a case worker, but...."

Toby's head now rested on Gus' shoulder and she slept peacefully for an hour or so while Myra poured out her heartbreak at having been deserted by the baby's father and rejected by her family. The old man listened quietly, prompting her onward with a frequent nod or an occasional m-m-hm, or a question like, "That doesn't seem very fair, does it?" or "What do you think you can do about that?"

At last, Toby woke, lifted her head, looked toward the sound of her mother's voice, and extended her arms to be taken. Myra welcomed her return, hugging the child to her breast.

"It's time for me to go home and feed her, Gus," she said, smiling wanly, yet pushing her hair back from her face in a gesture that bespoke a tad more confidence and pride. "Thanks for the shoulder. Toby and I both made good use of it."

"Any time," he said. "I can't do much for you but listen, but just remember, Grandpa Gus is always here for you.

"I will," she said, and as Gus watched her turn and walk away, he felt a heaviness in his heart for the difficult path this young woman had ahead of her. He wished there were a prescription he could fill for her that would lighten her load, unaware that he had already done that, merely by offering a friendly, uncritical ear.

THE ALMOST INSTANT HERO
Based on Pumice, Instant, Sheriff, Ravishing

Poker-faced Jeb Carter rode into Pumice, Arizona, expecting instant glory as the new deputy sheriff until he met Mae Doherty, his ravishing red-haired boss.

The major disciplinary problem in Pumice, you see, was also its major business enterprise, the White Rock Saloon, which was owned by Mae. Jeb expressed quite a lot of surprise about that when he first learned of it, but Mae explained it quite logically.

"Well, Jeb," she explained, smiling, "when I first came here as deputy under old Tom Potts, the place was a real squirrel hole. Filthy prostitutes, crooked card games, and gun fights made it a nightmare for poor old Tom. He just couldn't cope anymore, so he left it to me within a month."

Jeb looked her up and down from her crown of red hair, barely arrested into a loose braid coiled on top of her head, and grey eyes that held a glint of the sun in them, down the voluptuous column of her body, clad in sky blue chambray, to the toes of her white buck boots, wondering why in the Sam Hill anybody would hire her as deputy, much less leave her in charge of a town. But, as was his habit, he kept his thoughts to himself.

"The way I saw it," Mae continued, "the real problem was Wiley Hatch, the proprietor of the White Rock. If ever there was an evil man, a real emissary of the Devil, it was Wiley. So I decided, by hook or crook, to get rid of him and, being myself no mean gambler, I challenged him to a bet."

Noticing Jeb's lack of response to the story she was telling,

10

Mae paused and looked off into such distance as the White Rock allowed, and waited for an invitation to go on.

Jeb, being Jeb, just sat there sipping his beer as if he didn't care whether she did or not.

After a minute or so, Mae had him sized up and concluded her story with, "So, that's how I got ownership of the White Rock, and that's how I cleaned it up, and that's how come you get to come here and sit and drink beer and not have much to worry about."

Jeb's eyes moved off his beer glass, then, and looked up to watch Mae sashay off to visit with other customers of the saloon. Beneath his studied mask of indifference, he ached to chase after her and beg for the details she'd dismissed, but pride wouldn't let him. "What the Hell," he muttered. "She hired me to come here. She must need me for something. I'll just wait and see what happens."

He sat there, glowering after her for a couple of minutes more, then got up and started to leave. As he pushed his way through the swinging doors, though, he was met by the biggest man he'd ever seen. Maybe six feet four, he was, and a yard wide.

The man looked down at Jeb and made him feel like some kind of a bug. And like a bug, Jeb made a step to the side, letting the man pass, then scuttled off into the night.

But not very far. He went to the edge of the light cast by the windows of the White Rock, turned and stared back with a lethal glare.

He didn't know it, but his anger was not against the giant stranger. It was not against Mae. It was against himself because he wasn't the instant big shot hero he had expected to be. It was because Mae had seemed so on top of things, she didn't really need him.

Jeb stood there in the dark, feeling his impotent rage for a bit, then worked his way over to his horse, his gear still packed in the saddle bags. "What do you think, Sullivan? Shall we just light on out of here?"

It was just about then, though, that all Hell seemed to break loose inside the White Rock, and all Jeb could think of was that sweet little woman in there to cope with it all alone. Gun drawn, he crept up to the window and peered in. Sure enough, it was that big dude who was swinging this way and that, knocking everybody galley west. Mae stood on the stairway, white as a sheet, and helpless as a baby duck.

Jeb thought fast. He wasn't the biggest guy on the planet, but Sullivan was a pretty big horse. He leaped onto Sullivan's back, grabbed an axe that caught his eye, and sallied through the swinging doors, yelling at the top of his lungs and brandishing the axe around his head like a windmill in a gale.

By now, the stranger had Mae pinned to the balustrade at the head of the stairs. Jeb spurred his horse forward. They mounted the staircase like a hurricane. Releasing Mae, the stranger ducked the swinging axe and tumbled down the stairs like a giant sack of bones. Men below pounced on him, pounding him with fists and beer glasses and parts from broken furniture.

Wheeling his horse at the top of the stairs, Jeb caught Mae in his free arm and swept her up onto Sullivan's broad shoulders. Mae, with a great gasp of relief and gratitude, wrapped her arms around Jeb's neck and wept into his shoulder.

Jeb patted her back and, yes, violated his poker face with a very definite grin.

THE FABRIC OF FRIENDSHIP
Based on Quilting, Turnip, Hoard, Gathered

It was a sad day for the members of the Sew 'n Sew Quilting Society when their oldest member, dear little turnip-shaped Mable Dearborn, phoned to invite them to carry away the hoard of cloth remnants that she'd gathered over the years.

They all knew, as Mable did, that this day would have to come. At ninety-four, her hands were so knotted with arthritis and her eyes so dim with cataracts that she couldn't really practice her art any longer. Various of her friends picked her up to take her to their weekly gatherings, and though she could do little more than drink tea, munch cookies, and chat, they loved having her among them and hoped for surgery and medication to restore her skills.

Roberta Anderson, Mable's closest friend, became seriously alarmed at Mable's decision. "What's happened?" she wanted to know as she plumped herself down on the chintz-covered loveseat in Mable's cozy livingroom. "What's making you give up this way?"

Mable resumed her seat in her cushioned windsor rocker, leaned back, and smiling contentedly, closed her eyes. "Nothing's happened, Bertie. At least nothing bad. A little scary, maybe."

"What?" urged Roberta.

"I'm going to have cataract surgery, Bert."

"But Mable, that's wonderful. It's what you've been waiting for. You'll be able to see. Is this a time to give away your fabrics?"

Mable opened her eyes with a sigh and gazed at her friend. "I don't know how to explain this so it'll make any sense to you," she said. "It's just that.... Well, I've discovered that I don't really want to sew anymore."

Roberta remained silent for a moment, letting that idea sink in. "How did this discovery come about?" she finally asked.

"Well, when I came home from the eye doctor with this wonderful news, I began to think what it would mean – if all went according to plan, that is."

Roberta nodded, smiling expectantly.

"I would be able to read more. I would be able to enjoy my garden more. I would be able to see the faces of my friends more clearly. I would be expected to sew." She paused there, peering at the puzzled expression on her friend's face.

"Expected to sew?" asked Roberta.

Mable nodded. "That's just the way that statement appeared in my mind. I would be *expected* to sew."

"But ... but sewing and quilting has been the center of your life, Mable, for what, forty years or so?"

"Fifty, more like," Mable agreed. "I've loved it all. The feel of the fabrics in my hands, the fine needlework, the fitting, the matching. I found it so much more satisfying than machine sewing that my poor old Singer has been scarcely used in all these years."

"I know," said Roberta. "So why...?"

"I don't know, dear. Maybe it's a matter of energy. I still love going to the quilting meetings, being with all of you, enjoying your companionship, the little inside jokes, the gossip, the bitching."

"And we love having you there whether you sew or not."

Mable laughed. "I'm sure 'not' has been preferable to everyone since I've been so clumsy and blind."

Roberta laughed gently in agreement, but did not comment. "Is it your hands, Mable?" she asked.

"Probably. Hand sewing is so tactile, you know, but that part's hard to enjoy when you're hurting, and then, well, handling that little needle...." She broke off there, massaging her knobby fingers.

"I know," Roberta agreed, then fell silent, rubbing her own graceful hands in empathy. "But Mable," she said then, "If you give away your fabrics, it's like making an announcement. It's like saying you're not going to sew anymore, no matter what. That you're not one of us anymore. Do you see what I mean? It will make you feel like kind of an outsider in the group."

Mable nodded. "I've thought about that," she said. "The Sew 'n Sew's are my social center and I don't want to give that up."

"So why do it?" Roberta asked.

"Because not to is a lie," said Mable.

Roberta considered that carefully, then said, "No, dear, it's not a lie. It's just not revealing all of your feelings. And anyway, feelings change."

Mable thought a minute. "I suppose you're right, Bert, but I've already invited everyone."

"Well, uninvite them."

"They'll be disappointed."

"They'll be relieved that you've changed your mind. We're all very much concerned about you."

Mable smiled, then frowned. "They'll think I'm getting senile."

"Join the club," Roberta said, laughing.

"Not that one, thanks. I think I'll stick with the Sew 'n Sews."

Roberta smiled approvingly and nodded. "Good," she said. "Would you like me to call the gals for you and tell them you've changed your mind?"

Mable thought a moment. "No, dear," she said, massaging her gnarled hands and seeking her friend's face through misty eyes. "I haven't changed my mind about that. Those fabrics will never be used – at least not by me – and it hurts me to see them just sit there. I'd rather see them used by those who still can. Don't you see?"

Roberta looked again at Mable's hands and knew she was right. "Yes, Mable. Yes, I do see. I just didn't want to, I guess."

"Don't look so sad, Bertie," said Mable cheerfully, "After my surgery, I can enjoy seeing what others do with all those bits of goods. I might even make a suggestion now and then."

Roberta laughed. "I'll bet you will. You'll still be our Mable."

Mable joined her friend's laughter. "And I'll still be a Sew and Sew."

A LITTLE BIRD TOLD HER
Based on Robin, Windowsill, Gigolo, Strange

The robin who frequented Rosalie's windowsill tried to tell her that her handsome new lover, Pierre, was nothing but an unscrupulous gigolo, but alas, the naïve old maid could not understand his strange tongue.

Morning after morning, as the robin pecked at the bread crumbs Rosalie offered him, he twittered about the travails of other wealthy old women whose fortunes had been seduced by Pierre. Morning after morning, Rosalie listened intently, trying hard to divine his message. Something in the bird's voice and in his intense glance convinced her that it was important. Within a few minutes, however, the telephone would ring and Rosalie would hurry away to meet Pierre in some romantic place. Both the robin and his cryptic message were forgotten completely.

One day, as Rosalie and Pierre walked in the shade of the ancient elm trees of the city park, Pierre began telling Rosalie a sad story. It was the story of a little boy, torn from the arms of his mother and left to fend for himself in the streets of Paris. A little boy who grew to manhood, still searching for his mother.

"Now," Pierre told Rosalie, "I have at last located her. She has lived, all of these years, as the slave of a filthy barbarian. He no longer finds her useful, so is willing to sell her. But he wants much money in return."

"Oh, dear!" Rosalie exclaimed. "But surely that cannot be a great problem for one such as you, Pierre. I know little of your financial affairs, but you dress so beautifully and take me frequently to expensive restaurants and entertainments."

"Alas, what I spend on you is a mere pittance compared with the demands of my mother's captor," whined Pierre.

Rosalie laid a hand upon her breast in empathy with Pierre's distress, for she was kindhearted by nature and deeply moved by Pierre's story. "I have a little money put by," she confided. "Perhaps a loan...?"

"Ah, my dear one," breathed Pierre, "your words are music to my ears. I have come to hope, even, that once I could affect the freedom of my mother, I might persuade you to marry me."

Rosalie blushed and averted her eyes from Pierre, embarrassed that his confession expressed the fondest wish of her own heart. In doing so, she caught sight of her friend the robin, perched on a low branch of a mayberry bush.

Pierre, following Rosalie's gaze, spied the robin as well, and his face froze with consternation. He recognized the bird as the reincarnation of a young man whose mother he had duped out of her fortune, leaving them both in dire straits.

"Shoo! Shoo!" cried Pierre, flapping his arms at the bird, but the robin refused to budge.

Pierre picked up a fallen branch and attacked the robin even more violently, but the bird merely fluttered to a higher branch.

Rosalie stood in shock at this spectacle for a moment, but then clutched Pierre's flailing arm. "Pierre, Pierre!" she cried. "What ever is the matter with you? Why do you attack my dear little friend?"

Pierre whirled around, his eyes ablaze, and for a moment, Rosalie thought he would hit her. "Your friend?" he demanded. "Your friend? And does he talk to you? Does he tell you lies about me?"

"I – I don't know what he tells me," Rosalie stammered. "I can't understand his speech any more than I can understand your actions!"

Tears blinded Rosalie's eyes as she turned and hurried away, but the blindness that had shrouded her heart had lifted. She now knew. She finally understood what the little bird had tried to tell her throughout these past weeks. In gratitude, she stopped in at a pet shop on her way home to buy sunflower seeds. "No more crumbs for that dear, heroic robin," she thought.

Oddly, however, the robin never appeared on her windowsill again. She worried, at first, lest some harm should have come to him, but at last comforted herself with the intuition that she recognized as truth: his mission had been accomplished. He needed to go on to protect some other silly old woman. If so, she thought, smiling ruefully, I hope she will listen to him with her heart, not just her ear.

A MARTYR FREED
Based on Role, Shelter, Bright, Guilt

After ten years playing the role of martyr in a grubby homeless shelter for teenagers, the magic of a bright newsy letter from her daughter, Pat, lifted the mantle of guilt from Martha Martin's shoulders.

Yes, it was ten years ago, almost to the day, that Pat had left her mother a hate-filled note and disappeared. Reading that note again and again, absorbing the accusations of self-absorption and materialism, Martha accepted full responsibility for, first, the suicide of her husband, and now, the loss of her daughter. Without involving police, she spent several months in trying to locate Pat, constantly envisioning her in desperate, desolate circumstances. At last, she turned her attention toward trying to correct her own faults, trying to overcome her guilt and earn a right to Pat's forgiveness.

Selling the home she could no longer afford, she moved into a shabby apartment, and took a job doing cooking and cleaning in a nearby struggling homeless teen shelter, accepting little more than occasional meals in payment. Her personal appearance deteriorated until she looked worse than most of the clientele of the shelter, yet she took a perverse pride in her degradation. "Look at the devotion I give to these poor unfortunate children," she seemed to be saying. "No one can call me self-absorbed and materialistic now!"

In the process of all of this, of course, her old friends had dropped from her life, and her misery attracted only pity from her new associates. The years passed almost without Martha's notice, for she existed in a virtual fog of depression. Then came Pat's letter, forwarded to her at the shelter by an old friend.

"Dear Mom," it read,

I'm writing you in Mrs. Jennings' care, since my previous letter was returned to me as undeliverable at our old address. Perhaps it was just as well, for it made me think of you in a new light. Always before, I saw myself as having left you, as having punished you for not being the mother I thought I wanted. Now, I see you as having left me, or at least not being there for me to return to, and that didn't feel so good. It made me think.

You will be glad to know, I hope, that after floundering around for a while after I left home, I was led by the Salvation Army to finish high school, earn a scholarship, and go to college to become a teacher. Now, I'm teaching fifth grade in Orinda, have married, and am expecting my first child in four months.

Mom, I'm so sorry for the hurtful things I said in my farewell note to you, and I'm sorry it's taken me so long to realize how unfair I was. I hope you will forgive me and will write to me. Maybe, with the coming of this new life, we can make a new start.

Your long-lost daughter, Pat.

Martha crushed the letter to her lips and wept. Great, gushing tears of relief and joy flooded her eyes, and she felt an exaltation akin to what people seemed to describe in religious salvation. She herself had never experienced that, nor even wished it, but now knew that this letter was the reward she had sought for all of her years of penance and servitude.

She finished her shift at the shelter with a lightness of spirit that none of her co-workers had ever observed in her before. She smiled affectionately at the young residents and served their dinner with an unprecedented flourish. And then she went home.

It was as though she had just opened her eyes to a new surrounding. Not a shred of the opulence of her former home had followed her here. Even the homeless shelter showed more signs of comfort and love than did this barren little apartment. Having skipped dinner at the shelter, she opened the refrigerator to find half a loaf of bread, some processed cheese, and some limp celery. She thought of going out to eat, to celebrate, but the thought of doing so with no one to share it with filled her with an unutterable loneliness. She sat down at her small Formica dining table, buried her face in her arms, and let her tears flow once again.

After a time, Martha pulled Pat's letter from her pocket and reread it. Her fingers caressed the phone number at the bottom of the page. She wanted to call, but could not. Better to write, she decided. I can have more control over what I will say. She dug a pen and pad from a kitchen drawer and began: "Dear Pat." Then, after a long pause, began again on a new page. "Dearest Pat," then another long pause.

"How wonderful to hear from you after all this time, and to have all of your good news."

When no further words came for a while, Martha rose, got herself a drink of water, and made a trip to the bathroom. That seemed to open the gate to her heart, and she poured it out onto the paper. She wrote of her guilt and despair, of self-flagellation, of a numbness of spirit that had led her, she now realized, to become the pitiable, drab, unloving, unlovable kind of woman she had always despised. And whose fault was it? It was Pat's. Pat, that imperious, self-righteous little brat who had resented her efforts to recover from the loss of her husband and make a new life for herself. Pat, for whose sake she had devoted her life for the past ten years to a parade of kids just like her.

All of this, she spewed out onto the pages before her until her anger had vented itself and she sprawled, sobbing across the last page and, exhausted, fell into sleep.

When she awoke several hours later, she re-read what she'd written. A part of her wanted to fold it all up, stuff it into an envelope, and send it off. It will hurt her, she thought. It will give her a taste of the guilt I've felt all these years.

She went so far as to find an envelope and address it, to fold the pages and insert them. To seal the flap. To affix a stamp. Two stamps. It was a heavy missive.

She went to bed and tried to sleep, reviewing in her mind the tirade she'd committed to paper. Along about four-thirty, the first light of a beautiful spring day filtered through the dingy curtains of her room. She rose and stood at the window, watching the rosy glow fill the sky, and stayed there till her heart felt alight with this wondrous new day.

"I'm free!" she whispered to the growing light. "I'm free!" she said aloud as she lifted off her nightgown and stepped into her first shower in days. "I'm free!" she cried, smiling into her mirror as she saw her newly born self, her neatly brushed hair and rouged lips, her long-discarded green silk dress.

When she entered the kitchen, her eyes found the bulky envelope she'd left there the night before. She picked it up and read the address of her daughter. "I'm free," she said softly. "I don't need to mail this letter. I don't need to hurt my daughter." She turned on a gas burner and held the letter to its flame, let it flare, and dropped it into the sink to burn to ashes. In a few days, she thought as she watched it disintegrate, I'll write another letter. I'll tell Pat that I'm proud of her. Today, though, I have to take care of my own life. I have to take pride in me!

THE ENCHANTMENT
OF JAKE STARKEY
Based on: Azure, Moldering, Intrepid, Hovel

On a slight rise overlooking the azure beauty of Lake Paz stands a moldering hovel, whose deadly reputation serves to hinder exploration by even the most intrepid young hikers. It is said the now ugly structure was once a comely cottage, built by a silver miner named Jake Starkey for his lady love, Melinda Adams.

Jake, according to a newspaper photo that appeared in the *Coeur d'Alene Herald* back in July of 1879, was a malevolent-looking man. Fierce, bushy eyebrows shadowed cold, blue, deeply set eyes. A long, bony nose jutted from a wild black beard that all but obscured his thin, grim mouth. The face reflected not the joy of having staked one of the richest silver mines in Idaho, but the menace of a man who would protect his bounty by whatever means necessary. That picture, however, was taken before he met the beautiful Melinda, daughter of Hiram Adams, a multifarious trader who had recently settled in Coeur d'Alene.

Melinda was endowed with every asset that would tempt a man into marriage. Petite in stature, fair of countenance, graceful in manner, she presided over her father's elegant home with charm and efficiency. The frequent social gatherings demanded by Hiram's business dealings offered a perfect balance between luxury and informality. Guests, who included everyone from trappers fresh from the woods to railroad magnates and even, on occasion, the governor, felt a piquant combination of comfort and excitement.

It is not surprising to us, then, that when Jake won notoriety with his silver mine, his name found itself on the Adamses' invitation list. It was, however, a surprise to Jake. Essentially a loner, he came into town from his camp only for supplies and mail, rarely even stopping at the tavern for a beer, much less hob nobbing with the local gentry. Nevertheless, finding the prettily hand-written card in his post office box gave him a perverse pleasure. He suspected accurately that it was not himself, but his newly acquired wealth that Hiram Adams found suddenly attractive, yet some long-hidden heart string was gently titillated.

In the days leading up to the August evening, Jake made one concession after another in his grooming: He bought some new Levi's and the first chambray shirt he had ever owned. He bought new socks and underwear. A new hat and a red silk tie. Finally, though it was August and the weather hot, he had himself fitted with a finely tailored jacket. On the day of the event, he even visited a bath house for a thorough cleansing. Looking at himself in the glass, then, he considered his hair and beard, but drew the line at having it trimmed "It's taken me years to grow all this hair," he said to the attendant who offered. "People won't know who I am. Hell, I won't know who I am." He did, however, allow his mane to be shampooed and brushed into a semblance of civility.

At last, feeling like an actor on an opening night, he presented himself at the Adams house. Something, perhaps it was his new role, or this new stage, or the sheer charm and beauty of his hostess, brought out an aspect of his personality never seen before. He bowed. He smiled. He kissed her hand. He spoke eloquently of the romance of discovery, the lure of the deep wood, and the mesmerizing quality of Lake Paz. Melinda was captivated. At Christmastime, a wedding date was set for the following June. Hiram was ecstatic at the prospect of a wealthy son-in-law whose investments he could guide to his own advantage.

Thoroughly enchanted, Jake threw himself into the creation of his idea of a suitable home by the lake for his bride. So intent was he, that he and Melinda saw almost nothing of one another during that winter and spring. When he did go into town, it became clear to Melinda that the refinements that had attracted her to Jake during their brief courtship were but a thin veneer. Even his enthusiasm failed to disguise his true, uncouth nature. By June, the prospective bride was pleading with her father to allow her to decline this marriage. At last, he relented. The engagement was broken.

After his final meeting with Melinda, Jake went off toward his place at Lake Paz, and was never seen again. Gossip ran rampant for a time, but sympathy remained with Melinda, and few questioned what had happened to Jake. It was simply assumed that he was off prospecting for more silver, and perhaps that is true.

After a time, curious townspeople trekked out to the now abandoned cottage, which seemed almost to glow alongside the rude camp that Jake had called home. The door was left unlocked, but some strange aura forbade anyone from entering for a long time. Glances through windows, though, revealed luxurious appointments fit for a queen. Of the three known eventual trespassers, two, a young couple, both able swimmers, drowned when their canoe overturned on the perfectly serene lake. The third, a young man who had taken a silver teapot from the cottage as a gift for his sweetheart, suffered an immediate withering away of his flesh, and died shortly thereafter. Of course there was no proof of a direct connection between these trespassings and deaths, but it is believed that Jake still guards what was his with a vengeful hand.

Now, time, grime, and blackberry vines have obscured and rotted away the beauty that once graced the shore of Lake Paz, leaving this ugly hovel as a monument to improbable love.

A MATTER OF ETHICS
Based on: Nausea, Sprawl, Amoeba, Verdant

A wave of nausea swept over Natalie Balsam as she watched vellum drawings depict the agenda for the Olmstead Estate, a plan for housing to sprawl like a giant amoeba over its verdant acres.

She clutched her heart, remembering her lifelong love for this property. Sally Olmstead had been her dearest childhood friend. As seven-year-olds, they had donned Sally's dancing school costumes and, with Tchaikovsky providing terpsichoreal inspiration, had tripped a light fantastic over the terraced lawns that cascaded from the stately mansion that was her home. On other occasions, they'd perched like pretty birds among the branches of the ancient oak trees of the estate's woodlands. They'd munched cookies, sometimes eclairs or cream puffs provided by Maud, the Olmsteads' cook. In time, Natalie's family had left Mill Valley and the friendship had faded, but Natalie always treasured those memories.

Now, staring at the presentation by Bart Hume, the design director of her new employer, Elton Construction Company, Natalie felt horrified. In the first place, it had never occurred to her that the Olmstead Estate would not always remain as she remembered it. Yet, even if it could not, how could anyone think of replacing its beauty with this – this blight?

Cold sweat beaded on Natalie's forehead, her arms, her hands. She felt as though she might even faint, but forced herself to stay alert, to pay attention.

Now, Mr. Elton, Hank, as he liked everyone to call him, was smiling and shaking Bart's hand, congratulating the design team. He challenged the rest of the firm, including the drafts-people, of which she was the newest – to bring this project off with the quality of work it deserved.

Natalie shuddered anew at this, thinking what a travesty it was to use the word "quality" in connection with this – this blasphemy. Why, they were going to crowd twenty pseudo mansions onto the estate's seven acres. They would denude the hillside. There would be scarcely a blade of grass left, let alone a tree. The original house would be razed, deemed too old and impractical to be preserved.

When the meeting ended, Natalie retired to the restroom to wash her face and bathe her wrists – and to think. What can I do? she asked herself. I'm new here. I need this job to pay off my student loans. Heck, I need it to pay my rent. Still, as an architect – even a newly graduated architectural interne – she had a responsibility.

What's the worst thing about this, she pondered – aside from the fact that it's the Olmstead Estate? It's the denuding of the hills and the crowding in of too many houses. Too many, too large houses. Mr. Elton – Hank – has to be made to see that, and if no one else will stand up to him, I will.

With the courage one sometimes has when one's emotions are at fever pitch, Natalie walked down the corridor to Hank's office. His secretary was away from her desk, his office door was open. She walked in.

Hank raised his eyes from the papers on his desk and looked at her with mild surprise, but a friendly smile.

"Hello, Natalie," he said. "What can I do for you?"

Natalie wordlessly opened and closed her mouth a few times before she burst out with, "You can rethink the Olmstead Estate!"

Now, it was Hank's turn for speechlessness, but he finally chuckled patronizingly and said, "Oh, my! You seem to be upset about something, and I'm willing to listen for...." and here he glanced at his watch, "...five minutes. Why don't you just sit down and compose yourself?"

Natalie ignored the invitation, but stepped closer to his desk and bent her body toward him.

"How can you – a reputable builder, who's done good work all over Northern California, think of demolishing a beautiful site like the Olmstead Estate and cramming it with trite, trendy, useless houses that don't even have a prayer of becoming homes?"

Hank rose from his chair with such force that it crashed dangerously against the picture window behind him.

"Trite?" he bellowed. What do you know about trite? Is that a word they teach you in architectural school? Do you think you're a female Frank Lloyd Write now that you have your piece of paper hanging on your bedroom wall?"

"No! No, I don't, but I seem to be a better judge of land use integrity than you with your MBA!"

Hank stared at her, mutely fuming for several seconds before he took control of his temper and said coldly, "Miss Balsam, unless you want to terminate your association with this company, I suggest you turn yourself around, walk out of here, and never speak of this matter again – to me or to anyone else."

Natalie bit her lip in anger – at him, but even more at herself. She'd blown it, and she knew it. She turned and walked toward the door.

"Miss Balsam," said Hank as a parting shot. When Natalie turned to look back at him, he gave her a sardonic smile and said, "I'd also suggest you sign up for some post-grad courses in tact and diplomacy."

Natalie stared at him for a long, silent moment, then left the room, went to her work station, gathered her belongings, and left.

A week or so later, Natalie received a final paycheck and a letter of dismissal from Elton Construction Company. She was not surprised, of course, but felt renewed regret about her unceremonious departure. Her heart felt torn. She felt she's been right to speak her piece about the Olmstead Estate, but wished she'd thought it through more, been less emotional. Now, she'd accomplished nothing, and had lost her job to boot.

Amazingly, though, a couple of weeks after that, just when her hopes of further employment had reached a nadir, she got a call from Hank.

"I just wanted to let you know," he said, "that, mad as I was, I gave the plans for the Olmstead Estate a second look and decided you were right. Bart Hume has been let go. We're building a new design team."

"Oh, Hank!" Natalie exclaimed. "That's such good news!"

"I thought you'd be pleased," Hank said, then paused a moment or two before adding a second surprise. "Do you think you'd like to come back and be a part of that?"

Natalie's face flushed with joy and the phone trembled in her hand, but she tried to maintain some kind of dignity. "Why yes," she said calmly. "I think I would. I have a special interest in that property, and if–"

"Then I'll expect you tomorrow morning and we'll make a new start. Okay?"

"Fine," said Natalie, still trying for some semblance of cool, but then added, "And, Hank, I just want to say I'm sorry–"

"See you tomorrow, Natalie," Hank interrupted, and he hung up.

Natalie hugged herself and danced around the room for a minute or so, then paused to look out of her window at the green trees, bright flowers, and blue sky, and whispered, "Thanks."

A STAR COMES HOME
Based on: Ecstatic, Dramatic, Quietly, Fifty

Alone among the mainly enthralled observers of Bettina Anderson's dramatic return to her home town after fifty years, Harrold Strauss quietly sought to shed light on the marvel that she was still unwed.

Alton had yet to be discovered as a bedroom suburb of San Francisco back in the days when Bettina and Harrold had both attended highschool there, astounding everyone with their intelligence, talent, and physical beauty. Now its population had quadrupled and its property values soared, but it still retained the small-town qualities of friendliness, and pride in remembering some of the brighter lights among those who grew up there.

Bettina and Harrold were both honored in this way; pictures of them and plaques commemorating their accomplishments still adorned the main hallway of the highschool. Harrold, star athlete and honor student, served as studentbody president and brought fame to his school as a debater. Bettina, talented as both vocalist and actress, enjoyed equally starring roles among her classmates and in the community.

Once these two illustrious young people had graduated, no one was surprised when Harrold accepted a scholarship to Stanford, maintained his ties in Alton, and in due time came back a promising young attorney and civic leader who has been credited with guiding Alton's growth over the years.

Neither was it surprising that Bettina left for Hollywood shortly after graduation, full of promise for fame and fortune.

31

Even though, like so many promising young performers, Bettina was pretty much swallowed up by the hoards of Hollywood, the people of Alton remained loyal. Her proud parents kept them abreast of her small triumphs.

Foremost among Bettina's hometown fans was Harrold. His lovingly assembled scrapbooks chronicled their highschool years as sweethearts, and the sparse clippings of her since then. His diary recorded the stories of her related by her parents. He was silent in his adoration, but in all these fifty years, his fixation on Bettina had never wavered. Much of what he accomplished, he dedicated to her; he considered her his guiding light. She was the love of his life and he never took another woman into his heart, never married.

At last came the mid-July day when Bettina motored into town in a brave little fifteen-year-old white Porsche with Herb Alpert's Tijuana Brass blaring on the breeze that ruffled her short, Clairol-blonde curls. Everyone stared after her without the least idea who she was; everyone, that is, except Harrold. Harrold, observing Bettina's grand entrance from his second-floor office window, knew instantly from the flutter in his sixty-eight-year-old heart. A broad smile creased his withered face and brought a gleam to his tired old eyes.

Within minutes, Harrold's phone was abuzz with the news of Bettina's return; speculation as to where she had been and why she'd come back; plans for a welcoming soiree. Within days she'd been feted with dinners and cocktail parties, all of which Harrold avoided, and inundated with questions, most of which she adroitly dodged. Soon, though, like a burst of sky-rockets, full of brilliance and color and noise, the furor died, and Bettina settled into the little house left by her parents.

Curiosity remained and gossip ran its course as Bettina batted around town in her little white Porche. Harrold paid little attention to most of it, but clung with breathless hope to the rumor that she, like he himself, had remained unwed. Was there a possibility, he dared ask, that she had come back – for him? He longed to reach out to her, longed to go to her little house and knock on her door, but so many years of romantic retirement left him uncertain, so he did nothing but yearn.

Finally, a month or so after her return, Bettina put on a particularly pretty floral cotton sundress, a broad-brimmed straw hat, and white high-heeled sandals that displayed her plum-painted toenails. She mounted the stairs to Harrold's office and entered the reception room. Harrold's secretary announced her and ushered her in. The two looked at one another. Harrold stepped from behind his large mahogany desk and wordlessly took her into his arms.

"Why has it taken so long for you to come back," he asked. "I've waited for you all this time."

"I wanted to come back as a star," she said. "I wanted to light up your life. Now I know that will never be, but–"

"Bettina, Bettina!" Harrold groaned, "Don't you know that, to me, you've always been a star? You've always been the light of my life. You always will be!"

Fifty years, now, were as though they had never been, as Harrold and Bettina picked up the thread of their remarkable love story.

ALICE AND THE GUNNER
Based on: Balcony, Fiancé, Mingle, Bullets

Watching from a balcony overlooking the ballroom, Alice saw her fiancé, Senator Michael Davenport, mingle with the crowd in silky savoir faire, mount the podium to speak of world peace, then fall dead of bullets fired by a gunner from the opposite balcony.

Positioned as she was, Alice's glance had been attracted by the gunner's quick movements. "Michael!" she had screamed as the gunner fired, then dropped to the floor as she saw him aim a second round at her. Scrambling as quickly as her long satin evening dress would allow, she made her way toward the staircase she knew the gunner must use to escape, then paused behind a pillar, waiting for him to appear. When he did not come, she thought she'd missed him, and after a minute or two, proceeded, herself to the head of the staircase. She paused again, looking down, as the crowd boiled out of the ballroom into the foyer, trying with little hope to recognize the briefly glimpsed face of the gunner.

Suddenly, a gloved hand clamped over her mouth and yanked her backward. She stumbled and started to fall, but a steely arm grabbed her, held her tightly against a surprisingly soft, luxurious overcoat, but she felt a hard narrow prod pressing up under her armpit as her captor dragged her into a shadowy alcove.

"Just be quiet now, Mrs. Senator to have been. Don't fight me, you'll only get yourself killed."

The words came in a wet, hot, tobacco-stained breath against her ear. She cringed in repugnance and the move brought a brutal retaliation against her mouth and her rib cage.

Two security men had by now mounted the stairs, their guns drawn, their voices low. "The shots came from this side," Alice heard one of them say.

"Why wasn't somebody posted up here?" the other grumbled, as the two skulked off in the opposite direction from where Alice and the gunner were hidden.

Again, the wet whisper against Alice's ear. "The only way we're gonna get outta here is with your complete cooperation, little lady. You comprende?"

Alice nodded against the hand still clamped tightly over her mouth.

"Okay, then," he went on. "I'm gonna let go of you, and we're gonna walk down those stairs, and you're gonna act natural and take my arm like I was your best friend. You got that?"

Alice nodded again.

"Okay, now," he said, releasing her from his grip. "Here we go. No tricks, or a lot of people will get hurt, with you first on the list."

Alice leaned on the gunner's left arm as they started down the stairs. His right hand rode in the pocket of the black overcoat he wore. The crowd in the foyer below had thinned some, ushered out by security people, but those remaining raised their eyes to the couple on the stairs. Several, recognizing her, started toward her to offer comfort in this tragedy. Alice saw this and raised a hand, covertly signaling them to stop. They looked at one another in puzzlement, but complied.

The gunner was playing his part well. He composed his face into a perfect portrait of solicitous concern, and murmured mockingly sympathetic words close to her ear.

Alice appeared completely acquiescent to his attentions. The gunner allowed Alice to set the pace, and she moved slowly, as though in a trance. She leaned limply against him as they progressed a step at a time.

Three steps, four, five, then all at once Alice's head raised, her body stiffened, she grabbed the gunner's arm with both hands and sent him hurtling the rest of the way down the long stairway.

"Grab him!" she cried. "He's the assassin!"

But there was no need. The marble stairs had done all that was necessary.

As the stunned crowd stared helplessly at the spreading pool of blood on the foyer floor, Alice's friends rushed up the stairs to meet her, to take her into their arms.

"You poor dear," they murmured, and "I'm just so sorry," and "Are you all right?", but then, "How did you do that?" they wanted to know. "How did you have the nerve?"

I don't know," she said, and fainted

THE CURSE OF IDOLATRY
Based on: Solace, Cloven, Discus, Murmur

There was no solace for Demetre as he became aware of a murmur spreading through the crowd that his cloven feet must denote a supernatural factor in his superiority in the discus throw. Indeed, instead of the cheers he had hoped for, worked so arduously for, since he was a young boy of seven, there was complete silence as his championship was announced.

A few of his friends, boys who knew of his ten years' hard work preceeding this victory, gathered around him in congratulation, yet others clustered apart from him and eyed his strange feet.

An hour later, he entered the modest mud brick home he shared with his mother, Hermione, who welcomed him with a warm embrace and a celebratory goblet of chilled wine. Demetre accepted her accolades with a forced smile and entered the bath she had prepared for him.

As she sponged soothing, herbal water over his shoulders, he seemed to relax, but she knew his problem. She had attended the games. She had heard the talk. She knew, moreover, that this question of his cloven feet had plagued him since early childhood when he had first become aware of this difference between himself and others. He had asked her, time and again, but she had dismissed his questions, saying only that it was a mystery that, perhaps they would never solve, but that it would not keep him from his destiny.

When she had taken him, at age seven, to his first games, he

37

had said little,but began to emulate the discus throwers, seemingly entranced with the beauty of their motion. At first, he found it difficult because of his misshapen feet, but as he practiced, he became as graceful in his spin as a dancer. His arms and shoulders grew strong. He perfected his timing. He began to dream of this very day, when he would become the champion and quiet the taunts that besieged him. Now, that day had arrived, yet it was not at all as he had dreamed.

Hermione's eyes clouded as she gazed across the table at her son, picking at the extravagant meal she had prepared for him, and knew it was time to tell him the truth. She waited till he had pushed away his plate and sat staring into his empty hands.

"Demetre," she said, "I don't know if the story I have to tell you will ease your pain, but perhaps it will give you faith."

Demetre raised his eyes to her face and waited, emersed in his own misery, not much caring what she had to say.

Hermione saw this, but as one does when one believes that an immediate pain can bring eventual benefit, she began.

"It was almost eighteen years ago," she said, "that Dionysus came to our village, bringing with him the joy and celebration of life that was such a relief from Apollo's constant concern with reason and practicality. It was mainly we women who embraced him the most strongly. Our husbands, most of them clung to Apollo. My husband was one of those, and I, enchanted, rebelled against him.

"As perhaps you know, Dionysus could change himself into any guise he chose, and one day he circulated among the houses of our village as the most charming and handsome of men, playing melodies on his lyre that enraptured all of the women.

"'Come with me to the mountains, you dear creatures,' he said. 'You work so hard trying to please your men, you need a holiday. I promise you joy and refreshment from your harsh lives.'

"Well, large with child – with your birth imminent – I followed him. We did indeed go off into the mountains and for three days, forgot all of our sorrows and responsibilities. We drank wine, we braided vines and flowers into our hair, we sang and danced. Dionysus came among us, managing to make each of us feel beautiful and loved."

Demetre, by now, stared at his mother with such consternation that she feared she had made a mistake in telling him this story, but she believed so strongly that he needed to hear it, that she went on.

"It was just at this time, my son, that your father and most of the other men of the village came home from their war and found their women gone. Your father was a great favorite of Apollo, so he went to him and appealed to him for revenge against a woman who would abandon her home for revelry with Dionysus. Apollo reasoned that women, being the weak and witless creatures that they were, could not be blamed for their seduction by Dionysus. 'It is not your wife who should be punished,' he declared, 'but this upstart of a god!'"

"So then, you were not punished for your transgression," Demetre speculated.

"Not by Apollo," said his mother.

"But you were punished, and your punishment was that I should be born with the cloven feet of a Satyr," he guessed

"I'm afraid so, my dear son," said Hermione. "You see, Apollo and Dionysus entered into such a fierce exchange of retribution that the repercussions disturbed the tranquility of Mount Olympus and roused Zeus from his preoccupations. I don't know the details, of course, but I was told that he called Apollo and Dionysus before him, demanded to know what all the rumpus was about, and then pronounced the sentence that Dionysus must punish me, and that Apollo must mitigate the punishment."

"But Mother," cried Demetre in frustration, "it's not fair. I did nothing wrong, yet I have cloven feet, and now I understand that it is because of this that I have grown up without a father."

Hermione nodded, and reached across the table to take

Demetre's hand in her own. "But," she said, "it is the promise of Apollo that you shall succeed in any endeavor you undertake."

Demetre silently met his mother's eyes for a few moments before he pulled his hand away from hers, stood, and planted his hands upon his hips in an attitude of triumph. "Then I shall become as a god in the eyes of those who have abased me," he avowed.

"So be it," affirmed his mother, and as though this declaration had been endorsed by Apollo himself, the two of them heard the approach of a great horde of people.

Alarmed at first, Hermione and Demetre looked at each other with stricken eyes and held their breaths, but then recognized that the voices were filled with joy and adulation.

"They are coming to acknowledge you!" she exclaimed, and they both laughed in exaltation as they moved toward the door, but then Hermione stopped and gripped Demetre's shoulder with a firmly restraining hand. "Wait," she said. "A brand new idol cannot greet his idolaters with immediate and grateful acceptance of them. They must earn your love!"

It took Demetre a moment or two to compose his expression to one of appropriate dignity, then faced his mother for her approval. She nodded, and gestured for him to open the door and greet the crowd converging there before the steps of the modest mud brick house, bearing fruit and wine and wreaths of flowers and singing the praises of Demetre. When he appeared before them they prostrated themselves before him, then carried him off in celebration.

Hermione watched them go, raised her eyes to the heavens, where the sun was just completing its arc across the sky, and said, "Thank you, Apollo, I thought perhaps you'd forgotten."

And the voice of Apollo answered her. "Demetre has earned the adulation of the people by means of his hard work," said the god, "but the people think he is a god because of his cloven feet. If he has also wisdom, he can do great things. If he has not, he will lead the people in to an abyss and there is nothing I can do to stop him. That is the curse of the idol."

FALLEN ANGEL
Based on: Sinful, Pastor, Mercy, Fled

Reviving herself from a drowsy reverie concerning sinful thoughts of the handsome young pastor, Annabelle fervently asked mercy from her maker, drew her red woolen cloak closely around herself, and fled the chapel. She scurried down the street, then, oblivious to the falling snowflakes that whitened her hood and shoulders and made her path as slippery as her resolve never again to gaze lasciviously toward the form of the Reverend Archibald Combs.

Slippery indeed were her intentions, and she thought oftentimes of taking her prayers to some safer place, but found many excuses not to do so. She had grown up worshiping in this chapel. Her parents and friends would look askance at any change in her habit. It was convenient to her home. Most of all, she would feel at a loss to find God in some strange place.

All of these thoughts cluttered her mind as she made her way toward – toward where? she suddenly asked herself. She had, she supposed, meant to go home; at least she had no other conscious intention, yet she had turned in the opposite direction and would now have to turn back, with twice the distance to walk.

The snow continued to fall. It was an early, unexpected snowfall and she had not worn proper shoes for navigating the slippery sidewalks. As she progressed, the flakes grew smaller and icier, the pavement more slick. It took all of her attention to keep from falling. She did not notice when, once again, she passed the doorway of the chapel. She did not notice the dark form of the young pastor as he emerged and fell into step with her until he spoke her name.

"Annabelle," he said brightly. "May I offer my arm in support?"

Annabelle glanced up at him in surprise, blushing within the shelter of her crimson hood, and losing her concentration, fell like a brilliant autumn leaf at his feet.

Dismayed at her mishap, yet wanting to diminish any embarrassment she might feel, Archie quipped, "Well, I declare, a fallen angel in a red cloak!" as he knelt to her aid. "And a very pretty one, too," he added as she peered up at him, her cheeks ablaze.

"R-reverend Archie!" Annabelle stammered.

"Yes," he said, smiling mischievously, "and it appears that you didn't save much time by leaving the prayer service early."

"I-I was worried about the snow," Annabelle lied desperately by way of excuse as he helped her to her feet.

"As well you might, by the looks of things," he agreed. "May I see you home? Perhaps my clerical collar will ward off further evil."

Annabelle laughed shyly and took his proffered arm.

Later, as Archie and Annabelle sat before a blazing fire with her parents in their cozy sitting room, the two sipped hot chocolate and exchanged glittering glances from beneath protective eyelashes. As the years passed, Annabelle would remember little of what was said there that afternoon, but would delight, one day, in telling her grandchildren about the day their grandpa retrieved a fallen angel in a crimson cloak from a slippery path.

CON GAME
Based on: Chick, Chant, Oblong, Gamble

As innocently as a newborn chick, 84-year-old Alma Struthers sat ready to gamble her life's savings to Harry Wiggins' chant of promised riches, and at last handed him the fat oblong envelope that she'd clutched against her breast for nearly an hour.

Harry smiled unctuously and patted her hand. "You're going to be a rich lady, Alma," he said.

Alma returned his smile uncertainly, peering into his eyes and then riveting her glance on the envelope as he tucked it into the inside breast pocket of the brown wool suit he wore.

"Shouldn't I have some kind of paper?" she asked. "Some kind of receipt?"

"I could give you a receipt right now, Alma, but it wouldn't be worth the paper it was written on. I'm going to take this money right down to the Richland Investment Company and they'll send you stock certificates for the exact amount you've invested."

"But my husband always—" Alma began.

Harry cut her off. "This is entirely different, Alma. I'm sure your husband was never involved with anything like this, now was he?"

"Well, maybe not exactly, but—"

"If he was, my dear, there'd be a whole lot more money in this little envelope," and he patted the breast of his coat, over the hidden packet.

Alma nodded almost imperceptibly, her bespectacled brown eyes searching his green ones from under a corrugated forehead.

44

Harry, still smiling, gathered his hat and briefcase from beside him on the mauve velveteen sofa and rose to his feet. Alma rose as well, from her lavender platform rocker.

Harry extended his hand. "I congratulate you, Alma," he said. "You're going to be a very rich lady in a very short time. You have my card if you have any questions."

"Yes, Harry," said Alma, and then her glance shifted to a place behind Harry where two men in navy blue suits had suddenly appeared. Smiling brightly for the first time, she said, "Meanwhile, I'd like you to meet Mr. Conroy and Mr. Black from the FBI."

Harry spun goggle-eyed around, lost his balance and fell against the glass-topped coffee table, sending his floral china teacup crashing to the floor.

The two agents moved quickly to pull him to his feet, clap handcuffs onto his wrists, and read him his rights.

Harry cast an injured look among them all. "There must be some mistake. I'm here doing legitimate business with this woman." He looked sternly at Alma. "I was going to make you a rich woman."

"Yes, Harry, or whatever your name really is," said Alma. "Just like you did all of your other 'clients'."

"But how did you...." Harry began.

But it was Alma's turn to interrupt. "I've never learned much about doing business," she said, "but I know my husband always checked with the Better Business Bureau before handing over any money. I guess it's a pretty good idea."

DEATH AND RESURRECTION
Based on: Spectators, Widow, Mystic, Repeating

A goodly number of spectators, his widow among them, beheld the spectacle of Sam Gleason's burial as representatives of the mystic society that was his life began to rotate around the grave, each in turn repeating the subtle signals that no uninitiated person would recognize.

Sarah, Sam's widow, remembered, now, the evening, the first of many to follow, when Sam hurried through his dinner to attend, as he said at the time, "probably the most important meeting of my life." She was never to know the location or the subject matter of these meetings. Even now, she had no notion of the secrets or the purposes of these men who now paraded before her in solemn procession. All she knew was that for her and for her three teen-aged children, Sam was a missing entity.

Sam's law office had functioned as usual; money was never a problem, nor would it be now. Nothing, it seemed, would change, and that made her feel guilty. She wanted to, felt she should, feel some sense of sorrow, loss, anguish. She wanted to weep behind her widow's veil and felt ashamed that she could not; relieved that no one could see that she could not. Standing quietly beside her now-grown children, some ten feet or so from the open grave, watching the ceremony contrived by her husband's cohorts, Sarah did not even feel anger that the right to make these final arrangements had been usurped from her.

At last, the ritual at an end, she and her eldest son, Garrett, returned to the limousine that had brought them. They were taken

46

to a hotel where a wake had been arranged. She accepted a glass of champagne. Someone brought her a plate of food. One after another, various friends and relatives sat next to her, held her hand, kissed her cheek, searched for the right words. All had shared her extended isolation from Sam. All now shared the burden of acting and speaking appropriately. None knew how to touch Sarah's heart, to warm her.

Within an hour, all but Sam's secret circle had left the hotel, and Garret took Sarah home.

"Would you like me to stay?" Garrett asked when he had relieved her of her mink stole. "Is there anything I can do?"

Sarah, without answering, wandered into her living room and looked around as if it were new to her. She moved among its furnishings, touching a lamp here, a picture or figurine there. She sat in her accustomed chair near the fireplace and gazed at its vacant mate opposite her, as she had a thousand times over these years of Sam's involvement elsewhere.

"Mom?" Garrett prompted. "Is there–"

Sarah smiled gently, affectionately up at him. "Would you build me a fire, dear?" she asked.

"Of course!" he agreed. "Just the ticket!"

When the feeble flames began to gain strength and lap the light logs piled in the grate, Garrett perched tentatively in his father's chair. "How's that?" he asked.

Sarah smiled her reply. "I'm going to be fine now," she said, rising. I'm going to make myself a cup of tea. I'm going to feed that little fire. I'm going to stop grieving the loss of your father."

Garrett nodded his understanding with a quiet smile and settled more comfortably into the chair. "Bring me a cup too, will you, Mom?" he said. "It's time we all stopped grieving."

AN EVENING IN PARIS
Based on: Bedragled, Pocket, Sensual, Nozzle

Lost, exhausted, bedraggled, with one franc in her pocket, Lynette wandered the darkening streets of Paris, her sensual intake nil, until stung by the words of a stranger that hit her like a blast from the nozzle of a fire hose.

"I'll give you a bed if you'll be nice to me," the man said, his hand groping her bottom like a steel claw.

Lynette's eyes blazed open, her elbow jabbed reflexively at the man's solar plexus, and her legs suddenly found strength to carry her careering down the sidewalk and into a crowd of people waiting to board a tour bus, toppling a well-dressed elderly woman using a walker.

"Oh! I'm so sorry!" cried Lynette, dropping to her knees beside the woman. "Are you hurt? How can I help?"

"You've done enough," came the voice of a man behind her. "Why don't you watch where you're going?"

Lynette looked up at the man, her jaws working, trying to speak. "I was…. I was…." she managed before another voice, a sharp female voice, intervened.

"Never mind this little tramp," the woman screeched. "Someone get a doctor!"

"I'm a doctor," came a third voice, and a man dressed in chinos and a windbreaker pushed his way to the old woman's side.

The old woman smiled up at him wanly. "I think I'm all right, doctor," she said. "Nothing broken, but it'll take a derrick to get

48

me up."

The doctor smiled at her spunk. "You're sure now," he said, checking her pulse and her ankles. "Did you bump your head?"

"Just a little."

The doctor looked into her eyes and rotated her head, then looked up at the crowd gathered around them. "Let's give a little space here," he said.

Lynette, meanwhile, had righted the walker and now stood looking wretchedly down at the old woman, feeling totally helpless and unwanted there, yet unable to leave.

The doctor looked up at her. "Is there a seat attached to that walker?" he asked.

Lynette nodded and adjusted it into place.

"Do you think you can help me lift her?"

A man's voice from behind said, "I'll do it," and pushed himself forward.

"I think the girl can handle it," said the doctor, his eyes on Lynette's stricken face.

"I can," she said passionately, positioning herself to do so.

The doctor grabbed the walker and placed it behind the old woman, then he and Lynette lifted her and set her on the seat.

"Well! That wasn't so bad," said the old woman, and after thanking the doctor and accepting a glass of water from the proprietor of the cafe the tour group had just left, she turned her eyes on Lynette. "But you look like you need some attention, young woman," she said.

Lynette smiled uncertainly and looked down at her filthy clothes and broken shoes.

"We're going back to our hotel, dear," the old woman went on. "Why don't you come along and we'll see what we can do for you."

An unpleasant murmur issued from the crowd and Lynette glanced anxiously at the unfriendly faces and said, "I don't think—"

But the old woman interrupted her with, "Well, I do, and you knocked me over, so you have to do as I say."

Everyone boarded the waiting bus, then, and Lynette soon found herself in the old woman's room at the Hilton with an omelette, sliced tomatoes, and coffee before her on a small table.

"Now," said the old woman when Lynette had finished eating and they sat opposite each other, sipping coffee, "what has brought you to this deplorable state, my dear?"

Lynette smiled easily, now, feeling safe and fed and cared for for the first time in weeks. "It's not such an unusual story, perhaps, but I came here to write with a promise of publication and payment from my hometown newspaper."

The old woman raised her eyebrows in interest. "That sounds like a nice arrangement," she said.

"Well, it would have been, but the paper wanted the usual touristy pap about fountains and cathedrals and picturesque cafes and I was writing about the people I observed in the streets and what it looked like to be a struggling, unappreciated artist or whatever."

"They didn't want that?"

"Apparently not. They quit buying my stuff. I ran out of money and couldn't pay my rent, so my landlord kept my belongings and kicked me out. I didn't know anyone, so I just lived on the street."

The old woman peered empathetically at her young companion, wondering what she could do to help her. Outright charity was not her way – nor could she afford it.

"What have you learned about all those unappreciated artists?" she asked after a minute or so.

Lynette thought a bit. "Well, I just felt so sorry for them," she said. "I respected them for their dedication to their work and thought it was dreadful that they should live in such poverty. I wished there were a way to help them all."

"You're speaking of financial poverty," said the old woman.

Lynette paused to think and sip her coffee, then said, "Yes. Financial poverty. But after my own experience, I think most of them live in spiritual poverty as well."

"Do you think that has anything to do with their lack of success?"

Lynette paused again. "Probably so, but I hadn't thought of it that way."

"Do you think you live in spiritual poverty?"

Lynette bit her lip and looked out of the window, yet her thoughts were turned inward. "Perhaps so," she said at last. "At least I have in these past weeks. I couldn't think past my next meal and my next night in some doorway."

"What do you want to do now?" asked the old woman gently. "Do you want to go home?"

"No!" Lynette exclaimed more loudly than she'd intended.

The old woman exaggerated astonishment at this small outburst and smiled, but remained silent.

"I want to stay here. I believe I've learned something, gained some insight. I think, now, I can really write something meaningful about these people – even about my own story – and that it might have some value. Maybe to my hometown paper, but if not...." She shrugged. "But it's unrealistic to expect someone to support me while I do that, and somehow I have to eat and be safe and clean."

"That sounds like you need to earn some money."

Lynette nodded and looked down again at her clothing.

The two were quiet for a time. The old woman again wondered how best to help this girl; Lynette eyed the extra bed in the room and wished the old woman would invite her to use it.

At last, the old woman spoke. "Why don't you have a bath and spend the night here with me. In the morning we'll have breakfast and find you some presentable clothing."

Lynette's eyes brightened with pleasure, even as her face flushed with embarrassment, having her silent wish come true in this way. At a loss for words, she leaned forward in her chair, clasping her hands as in supplication, and saying, "Oh, but … but, really, that's so–"

The old woman understood the girl's confusion and approved of it. "As a matter of fact," she said, " I'm going to be here for the rest of the week and you're welcome to share my room and meals with me. That will give you four days."

Lynette clapped her hands to the sides of her head as though to keep her brain from reeling out of control. "I'll find a job!" she exclaimed. "I'll have a new start!" And then, tears glistening in her eyes, came her barely audible "Thank you."

"You're welcome, dear," the old woman said.

Later, when both had bathed and lay in their fresh, soft beds, with the sounds and lights of the Paris night finding their way through their curtained windows, they bid each other good-night. A few minutes passed and then Lynette, sensing that the old woman was still awake, said, "You know, I'm still so sorry that I knocked you down, but I'm awfully glad I ran into you."

The old woman laughed quietly. "Me, too," she said.

BLIND FAITH
Based on: Shrouded, Pond, Master, Cubit

The sea, shrouded in a heavy cloak of fog, lay calmly as a pond, yet the launch, unbidden by its master, began to rotate, cubit by cubit in a counter-clockwise direction. It was as though some unseen hand controlled the motion of the boat, for the sails hung slack, and adjustment of the rudder had no effect at all.

Captain Sandor stood perspiring in the dank, cold midday gloom, feeling helpless. He thought of his six-man crew, standing silently, gazing out at the nothingness around them. He thought of his mission, the secret transport of a magical potion that would appease the king of the Faventines and avert a threatened war.

The fog, this calm, had halted their progress across the Arnian Sea and now this unguided motion would lose their bearings altogether. Nothing in all of Sandor's long experience had prepared him for this.

He called his men together and said to them, "You can see, my friends, that we are helpless here. We have no wind, and now we have no control over whatever mysterious force it is that moves us."

The men stood silently around him, waiting for him to go on. Waiting for him to tell them of some plan. He was their captain. He always knew what to do.

Sandor looked into their expectant faces, recognizing their trust in him, and said finally, "Just as you have faith in me, my lads, I must sometimes rely on some wisdom greater than my own. I must sometimes admit that I am without power to guide my own ship."

The men shifted their feet and looked around them, but remained silent.

"I'm going to ask you to place your faith, along with mine, in that higher power," said Sandor, and bowing his head, he dropped to his knees on the fog-damp deck.

The men followed his example and the seven of them remained there until, all at once, they felt a breeze. They looked up and saw that the sails were swelling softly. The fog was lifting. Warm sunlight filled their eyes. The launch was progressing through the water as though guided, even though Sandor had not touched the tiller, and soon they sighted land. Sandor looked through his spy glass and saw that it was not their intended destination, but found he was still powerless to change course.

When they landed, a few hours later, they were met by a delegation of the very people to whom he was supposed to deliver the potion.

"How did you know to come here instead?" they wanted to know. How did you avoid the ambush set for you?"

Sandor smiled and looked around at his men. "We had a very good navigator," he said.

LETHAL SCHEMES
AND APPLE BUTTER
Based on: Sharing, Butter, Tamper, Lichen

One Thursday afternoon, as Claudia and Angela sat in their parlor sharing scones and apple butter, they sought a catchy scheme to tamper with the longevity of Claudia's lichen-like husband.

Both of these sisters, though they were loath to admit it, and their careful grooming and jaunty demeanor belied it, had entered their eighties several years before. The only thing that made them feel really old was the intrusion in their lives of Ezra, who sprawled in his recliner chair – right there in the middle of everything – and either snored or stared sourly at nothing in particular and sucked his teeth.

Neither of them was, herself, capable of any sort of actual violence toward the old geezer, but they each made a game of trying to incite the other toward finding some kind of final exit for him.

Removing them still another step from direct address to their problem was the fact of Ezra's constant presence in the room as they discussed it. Thus it was that they couched their conversation under the guise of murder mysteries or news articles they'd read – or sometimes simply invented.

"Did you think it logical," Angela might say, for instance, "that Scotland Yard could actually trace the arsenic to that obscure diamond merchant?"

And Claudia might reply, "No indeedy! There didn't seem any

55

connection at all. Once Lord Lipton was dead, who was there to say that it was Lady Lipton who had invited that man to tea?"

"And who could know that Lady Lipton had left the man alone with her blind husband so that he could poison the tea," Angela might add.

Claudia might then cock an eye at Angela and say, "Hm-m-m. That reminds me. Weren't you going to ask that herbalist over to tea sometime?"

"I don't think so, dear," Angela might say, "but I do think it a delightful idea. She might have a remedy for that complaint you've been speaking of."

Claudia's gaze might then rest thoughtfully upon her husband for a few moments before she'd suggest, "You know her better than I do, Angela. Why don't you ask her?"

But of course, nothing would come of it, for it was, after all, just a game they played.

On the particular Thursday of which we speak, it was a news article that guided the chat.

"Wasn't it dreadful the way that woman died in her bathtub when her hair drier fell into it?" asked Claudia.

"Dreadful!" agreed Angela. "Things like that do happen, though, I suppose. People do like to use electrical appliances while bathing, even though they're warned and warned."

Claudia shuddered. "Let's not talk about that anymore, Angela. I can't bear to think of it."

Angela glanced sidewise at her sister. "Well, you brought it up, dear. Don't blame me." A small silence ensued before Angela spoke again. "Don't you keep a small radio – the plug-in kind – on a little shelf over Ezra's bathtub, Claudia?"

Claudia met her sister's eyes and blinked. "Well … yes, but there's no reason it should fall in … is there?"

Suddenly the women's attention was drawn to Ezra, who was sitting bolt upright. His mouth had fallen open, his glassy blue eyes stared fiercely at his wife, and his clawlike hands clutched the arms of his chair as though to squeeze the life out of them.

"You women! You nasty, nasty women!" he croaked. "Do you think I don't know?"

Claudia stared back at him. Bright red splotches appeared on her cheeks. Her eyes welled up with tears. Her speechless mouth opened and closed like a gasping tropical fish.

Angela, outside the beam of the old man's lethal stare, was less affected by it. "Ezra!" she cried. For Heaven's sake! What's got into you?"

Ezra shifted his gaze momentarily to Angela and then slumped back into his chair. His clutching hands relaxed, his chin found its resting place on his chest, his eyes closed for the last time.

Claudia started from her chair. "Ezra!" she sobbed. "We never meant...." And then she fell forward into a faint from which she never completely recovered.

Angela has assumed the role of caregiver for her sister since then, for Claudia has become as lichen-like as Ezra had been. Like Ezra, she insisted on spending her days in the parlor – right there in the middle of everything – either dozing or glaring at anyone who might enter the room.

This has made for a dismal life for Angela, but nevertheless, apparently having derived some kind of moral message from this calamity, she's changed her choice of nourishment for her fantasies from murder mysteries to romance novels – except for now and then when she sits in the parlor munching scones and apple butter, listening to Claudia suck her teeth.

THE MAN IN
THE LAZY ACE SALOON
Based on: Wobbled, Snort, Misuse, Biped

When Jake Logan wobbled up to the bar in the Lazy Ace Saloon and ordered a snort of rye, Will Smithley thought it would be a misuse of the word to call this biped a man. Nevertheless, Jake held Will's attention. He was a writer, you see, and had come here to the little town of Boulder Creek to pick up some background for a new novel he had in mind.

It wasn't simply Jake's unkempt attire that caused Will's assessment; several of the men sitting around drinking beer and playing pool and poker were dressed almost as shabbily. None of them, however, had Jake's greyness of complexion or the sad, beaten look about the eyes. None of them appeared already drunk enough to fall down before ordering a drink – and hard liquor at that.

Most puzzling of all was the manner in which Sal, the bar tender, greeted him and served him without so much as a glance at his apparent condition. Neither did the other men seem to take notice of anything unusual. Moreover, when Jake had downed his rye, hitched his small frame onto one of the high stools lining the bar, and ordered a beer, a couple of guys went over to join him.

"Hi there, Jake," said one. "How's it going, old buddy?"

"Oh, not so good, Howie," Jake answered. "It's just this damned weakness that gets me. And I have no coordination left at all."

"You seemed to handle that shot glass pretty well," laughed

the second man.

Jake winked with a wry smile. "Reflex, Charlie," he said. "Don't need coordination for that."

The two friends laughed comfortably, took stools on either side of Jake, and set their beer mugs on the bar.

Jake used both hands to pick up his own mug, and they shook so with the effort that he spilled some beer down the front of his shirt as he brought the glass to his mouth. His two friends glanced at each other with sorrow.

Will, sitting alone at the other end of the bar, busied himself with cracking and eating peanuts. He tried to be unobtrusive as he watched the others, reflected in the mirror, but at the same time, wondered how he could learn Jake's story.

When Jake after a half-hour or so struggled from his stool, bid his friends good-bye, and staggered back into the sunlight of the quiet street of this little old logging town, his friends sat silently, watching him go.

After a minute of so, Will called to them. "Can I buy you guys a beer?" he asked.

Howie and Charlie looked at him, and then at each other, and then Howie spoke. "Sure," he said, "why not?"

Will got off his stool and took one next to Charlie, the nearer of the two, and they all ordered fresh beers.

"New in town, aintcha?" Charlie asked.

"Brand new. Just got here an hour ago," Will told them.

"Lookin' for local color," I s'pose," suggested Howie.

Will looked embarrassed, but admitted it was so.

"You a writer or somethin?" asked Charlie.

Will nodded.

"Well, you won't find much color around here," Charlie said. "Just working men who mind their own business."

"Right," Howie agreed.

"The color, if you want to call it that, is out in the woods where the work is. You won't learn much just sittin' here in the saloon," Charlie chided.

"And even in the woods, why, it takes months – even years – to learn much," Howie went on, and Charlie nodded in agreement.

Will smiled and broke open a peanut. "I'm sure that's true," he said, "but – well – that guy who just left. Who is he? What's his story?"

Howie and Charlie looked at each other again, but remained silent for a few seconds.

"Don't know's we want to talk to you about him," Charlie said. "He's our friend. Used to be our boss. He's got Lou Gehrig's. The rest you have to live through to know about."

"But...." Will began to argue.

"Thanks for the beer, Mr.," Howie said, and, as one, the two men slid from their stools, waved good-bye to Sal, and left the saloon.

Will sat where he was for a while, nursing his beer and munching peanuts. He hadn't learned what he'd hoped, but he'd witnessed something perhaps even better. Something about pride and loyalty among men who work together at dangerous jobs. Something about the value of privacy. And he'd learned that that little "biped" who'd entered his life an hour ago was indeed a man. A man he'd never forget.

A PRINCESS MEETS REALITY
Based on: Adapt, Daisy, Concur, Ermine

Princess Margetha, accustomed to wearing diamonds and ermine and receiving roses from princes, knew she must adapt her attitude to concur with current circumstances as she accepted a single daisy from an admirer.

Looking forward to becoming queen one day soon, you see, Margetha had decided that in order to rule her subjects with objective compassion, she needed to learn what it was like to walk in their shoes. With that in mind, she sent out word that she would be visiting a foreign country for a time – which, in a sense, was true. Then, disguising herself as a simple country girl, she made her way to a fair-sized industrial city to look for work.

Now, Margetha had been educated, of course, in the arts and sciences and languages. She had gained skills that country girls, in those days, did not even dream of. On the other hand, she lacked the training that would have been second nature to a country girl, such as spinning, weaving, and sewing; skills that would fit her for a job in a factory. She had learned to embroider quite nicely, however, so she took some samples of her work to a maker of fine linens and was hired immediately.

To her surprise and dismay, she was set to work in a dim, cold building among twenty or so other women of varying ages, and given a large bundle of napkins to monogram with the crest of her very own mother, the queen.

Margetha picked up a napkin, sorted her silks, and began to stitch in the leisurely manner she had always employed for such

61

work. She paused at frequent intervals to rest her eyes and to consider the women around her. How can I, she wondered, effect improvements in this environment that would make their lives so much more pleasant? Her supervisor soon let her know that none of this was acceptable.

"Just where do you think you are," cried the bent little man, who carried a slender cane with which he gave her a sharp whack across the shoulders. "Do you see the way these others are working? Do you see the way their fingers fly? Do you see the way they keep there eyes glued to their tasks?" Margetha nodded solemnly and he went on, "Well, that's what I expect of you, girl. This is a factory. It's not a sewing circle."

Margetha winced at the pain inflicted by his words, as well as by the cane, and tried to work faster. Hours passed. Her eyes grew bleary. Her neck, her back, and her wrists began to ache. Her fingers cramped. Tears fell on the napkin she was working, and, *Whack!* Another blow from the cane fell across her shoulders.

"Get out!" cried the little man. "We need workers here, not cry babies!"

Margetha set aside her work, her face aflame with anger and embarrassment. She glanced around the room at the other women, hoping for some solicitude from them, but found none. Some of them raised their eyes to her as she passed them, but they held only cold affirmation of the supervisor's appraisal.

Making her way to a nearby park, Margetha sat on a bench in the early evening light, pondering her situation. She had no money. She had expected to be paid. She should have been paid, for she had worked for seven hours. "That's right!" she said to herself. "I should have been paid and paid I shall be!"

She retraced her steps to the factory and confronted the manager who had hired her. "I admit that I could not work as fast as the others," she said, "but I did work for seven hours. I completed six and a half napkins. I deserve to be paid."

The manager looked at her with a fishy stare. "Who do you think you are, barging in her and talking to me like that?"

Margetha considered revealing her identity then and there, but decided to persevere in her disguise. "I am a person who sold you my time and my skill," she said. "I expect to be paid for it. If not, I will go to the queen herself and let her know the kind of man she does business with."

The manager laughed harshly. "Go ahead, you little bumpkin," he said, and he turned his back on her.

Margetha just stood there, tapping her foot audibly on the barren floor. Tap, tap, tap, tap, tap, on and on for several minutes.

The manager glared at her. "Leave!" he shouted.

"I will not!" she said coolly but emphatically, without interrupting the rhythmic tapping of her foot. Tap, tap, tap, tap, tap....

"All right!" cried the manager after another ten minutes or so. "You say you completed six and a half napkins. I will will pay you twenty-five cents each."

"But that's only a dollar and sixty-two and a half cents," Margetha protested. I was to be paid three dollars an hour. That would be twenty-one dollars."

"Quite the little mathematician, aren't you," said the man with a sidewise glance. "Who are you?"

"Just an honest country girl trying to make her way in the world and expecting those I work for to be honest too," she said.

The manager smiled in a conciliatory way and said, "Tell you what. You worked seven hours but you didn't produce enough to be paid full price. I'll meet you halfway. Ten-fifty. That's my final offer."

Margetha thought for a few seconds and decided it was fair. "I accept," she said.

It was quite dark by the time she stepped back into the street and she stood still a moment, looking around her, wondering where to go. A young man, a clerk who had observed the whole exchange between Margetha and the manager, came out of the building and stood beside her.

"You acted like a princess in there," he said, and she smiled. "It's getting dark. Can I walk you somewhere?" he asked.

"I must find food and lodging," she said. "I just arrived this morning."

"I know of a boarding house not far from here," he said. "I'll take you there."

Margetha thanked him, and as they walked together, she asked him questions about his life and work at the factory, and made mental notes about what conditions could reasonably be improved. She thanked him again when they arrived, and he tipped his hat to her, and bid her a good night. As he turned away, he noticed a hedge of Marguerites growing beside the house, picked one, and offered it to her.

"For you," he said with a shy smile.

Accepting a simple daisy from a commoner was another experience from which her royal life had protected her, but it spoke of the goodness of the people she would someday rule. The day had been a bitter lesson, but she believed she'd be a better ruler for it. This young man's kindness, and this daisy, made her glad of that.

REMEMBERED ROMANCE
Based on: Thumbed, Exile, Flavor, Arrow

As I thumbed a photo album from forty years ago, memories of an almost forgotten love came out of exile and brought with them the peppermint flavor of a kiss that had made my heart a target for Cupid's arrow.

The picture before me showed the two of us, Gordon and me, at a dance. We had just won the Viennese waltz contest and had been given, as our prize, a bottle of champagne. We had never even met each other before that evening. It was a singles' dance, you see, and each of us had attended alone. The dancing itself had been as thrilling as the winning of the contest, for we had moved together, responded to the music together, as though our very souls were one. That unity stayed with us for the rest of the evening, as we experienced together the myriad rhythms that comprise American dance music.

Afterward, he took me home in a battered blue convertible that, to me, was as grand as a limousine. When he walked me to the door of my apartment building, he carried our bottle of champagne along with him, and I anticipated with a mixture of fear and excitement that he expected to be asked inside. My mind, though it was as fizzy as though we'd already drunk the champagne, said no. We had spent the whole evening together in the intimacy of the dance, touching, responding, sharing, and yet I knew virtually nothing about him. Still, my heart wanted to cling to this moment, afraid to let go, afraid there might never be another.

I rummaged in my hand bag for my key and tried to think. We reached the door and stood in a pool of dim light. He took my key from my hand, unlocked the door and held it open for me.

"Thanks," he said, "I don't know when I've had more fun."

"Me too," I answered, confused. It was as though we were still dancing and I felt, for the first time, unsure of his signals. Why was he carrying the champagne if he didn't mean to come in and share it with me?

It was time for me to think for myself. I stepped through the doorway and turned to face him. "Thanks for bringing me home," I said with a smile that probably looked a little too bright.

"I'd like to see you again," he said, "and get to know you.

"Me too," I said again, as if my vocabulary was limited to those two words.

He handed me the champagne. "Why don't you put this in your fridge for the night, and tomorrow I'll pick up some sandwiches and we can go on a picnic in the park – that is, if you're free."

"That's a marvelous idea," I enthused, and then, trying to sound a little cooler than I felt, added, "I can be free after one o'clock."

"Perfect," he said, stepped up into the doorway with me, and kissed me softly on the lips. I had never cared much for the taste of peppermint – until then. I had rather objected to people who chewed gum at all – until then. I had been a sensible woman, too cautious to ever really fall in love – until then.

All night long, I relived the evening that was and anticipated the day that would be. The days and nights and years that might be. I paused now and then, warning myself that if I did not get some sleep, I'd be a wreck in the morning, but sleep would not come.

I rose at about eight and looked into the bathroom mirror at the prophesied wreck, opted for a long bath instead of church, washed my hair, shaved my legs, polished my nails, and ironed an ankle-length floral cotton skirt and an off-shoulder blouse. Another look into the mirror won approval. I dug out a picnic basket I'd never used, washed its plates, and ironed its napkins. I wrapped the champagne in an embroidered tea towel and tucked it into the basket together with a pair of crystal goblets, an apple, an orange, a banana, and some cookies I'd baked a few days before.

The doorbell rang at one fifteen. I pressed the release button for the foyer door. A few seconds later, he stood before me, handsome as ever, but the energy that had existed between us last night was absent. One can never explain such things, one just knows they are so.

We looked at each other and smiled, both of us trying to bring back the magic, believing that if we simply went forward, we would find it again. We exchanged a few words. I handed him the picnic basket. We walked down the stairs and got into his car. Neither of us could think of anything to say, we just sat there looking at each other.

"Look," I said after a minute or so, "we really don't have to go on with this."

He nodded sadly and took his key out of the ignition. "I'm sorry," he said.

"Me too," I said, and we both smiled.

He got out of the car and came around to help me out of the car with the basket.

"I'll call you," he said, but of course we both knew he never would.

I closed the album and looked fondly across the room at my husband. "You know, honey," I said, "I'm so glad you don't chew gum."

He looked up from his newspaper to give me a quizzical look, I blew him a kiss and closed the album with a contented sigh.

THE TWAIN SHALL MEET
Based on: Celery, Sporty, Maxim, Humor

When Adriana, with her celery stalk looks and emery board sense of humor, told me she would marry sporty, amiable Dave, it seemed to prove the maxim that opposites attract.

I had known Adriana for years and, although I'd always admired her cool poise and well-groomed beauty, and often laughed at her acerbic observations of the world around us, I could never feel close to her. I always felt a little more aware of my own imperfections while in her presence, fearing lest her caustic judgement might turn its eye on me. That we had remained friends at all was rather remarkable, and yet I felt an irresistible attraction to her, as, apparently, she did to me.

I was with her when she met Dave at a coffee given for a political candidate we both favored, but of whom she'd asked some biting questions. Dave came up to us after the formal part of the gathering had ended, and chided Adriana for having been put in her place by the candidate's adroit answers. Adriana smiled and said, "Yes, I was sure he'd do that. I wanted to help him show his mettle."

The expression on Dave's face changed, then, from challenge to conspiracy, and the two of them became engaged in an earnest discussion of the issues involved, and the chances of this candidate to win the election.

I added little to the conversation, but observed Dave carefully. He was of average height, a tad shorter than Adriana, and had a soft, almost pudgy quality about his face and body that seemed incompatible with Adriana's slender firmness. His eyes, when he was teasing, and now, even in serious discussion, radiated a friendly warmth and his smile was natural and easy. There was earnestness in his expression, but no anger or tension, whereas Adriana's face reflected a sternness that spoke of constant criticism.

The party began to break up around us. I looked at my watch and reminded Adriana that I needed to pick up my son from soccer practice in a few minutes. She nodded and her eyes met Dave's with the most genuinely searching look I'd ever seen her give anyone.

"I have a book you might like to read," he said, and I thought, yes, Dave, I'll bet she will read almost any book you offer her.

Adriana opened her neatly organized handbag and took out her card case. "I'll give you my card," she said. "You can call me."

Now, three months later, I look at Adriana as she tells me of their wedding plans. There is no obvious change in her appearance, and her observations are as acute and lethal as ever, but she laughs more. When she looks at me I feel a new warmth in her gaze. A relaxation in her attitude.

At last, after all these years, I feel as though we are truly friends. I can accept her invitation to be matron of honor at her wedding with confidence and love. It seems that opposites can not only attract, but sometimes learn from one another.

TRIANGLES
Based on Lithe, Wiped, Exhort, Affirm

Night after night my brother Billy and I would exhort our mother to make our sister Lillian help with the dinner dishes, night after night she would affirm the justice in our exhortations, yet night after night saw Lillian's lithe figure skip off to the family's recreation room to practice her ballet exercises while Billy washed dishes and I wiped.

That Billy washed all the time while I was stuck with wiping and putting things away was a thorn in my side as well, but he was ten and I was only eight. It was just kind of understood that he should be the boss and choose the job he liked better. Moreover, both of us were sick of the way six-year-old Lillian was treated like a little princess while we did all the chores – one of which was looking after her when Mama was not feeling well. It made for a bond between Billy and me that was a great comfort to me, so I didn't take a chance on messing it up by complaining.

For me, it wasn't simply that Lillian was the adored baby of the family and was given the dancing lessons that I'd always wanted. It was that she really was cuter and daintier and funnier than I'd ever been. She was agile and energetic and quick, while I'd always been kind of a lump. For these reasons, my resentment of her was deeper than Billy's and more intractable. Billy, when all our grumbling was done, would tease Lillian and play with her and laugh with her, leaving me out. I felt like a non-person and took to going off to a little nook under the stairs where I could be alone to read or draw pictures, or daydream. A place where in my imagination I could be some kind of star and make everyone admire me, pay attention to me.

A couple of years passed in this way and then Mama's illness become chronic and she was confined to bed.

"Marcia," Daddy said to me, "We're going to have to depend on you to be a big girl now and look after your little sister after school. We'll have a woman to come in and tend to Mama's needs and do some cleaning and cooking, but she'll be here for only a couple of hours a day and won't have time to pay much attention to you children."

I nodded and truly meant to do my best. It didn't even occur to me to wonder why it was I, not my older brother, who was given this job. Billy was a boy. That was that. Besides, I saw this as an opportunity to be a kind of heroic figure in this family for once.

Looking after Lillian, however, was a bigger job than I'd expected. She was angry because her dance lessons were interrupted, there being no one who could drive her across town twice a week, and angry because I was "boss of her." She learned early on that if she did something destructive or dangerous, it was I who got scolded for not doing my job well enough. Almost every day, therefore, she'd make a mess or break something or run off somewhere and not allow herself to be found until Daddy came home.

One day she found a way to climb up onto the roof of our one-and-a half-story house.

"What are you doing up there?" I cried when I saw her. "How did you get up there?"

"It was easy," she crowed. "It's fun up here."

"Well, come on down," I ordered. "You'll break your neck."

"No. Watch!" she shouted, and did an arabesque on the very ridge.

"Lillian!" I screamed in terror as I saw her lose her balance, topple, and disappear.

"Please God, please, please," I prayed as I raced around the side of the house. I reached the front lawn to find her sprawled awkwardly at the base of the plum tree, a broken branch of blossoms beside her. Mama stood on the porch in her nightgown, screaming.

Our next-door neighbor came through the hedge and surveyed the scene. "You take care of your mother," she said to me as she knelt down next to Lillian. "And bring me a blanket," she added over her shoulder.

I stood there petrified for a second or two, then finally, as though in a trance, moved up the steps toward my mother. She had stopped screaming, but stood gaping at the scene on the lawn, her hands clasping her face. I wanted to put my arms around her, needed hers around me, but was afraid to touch her. She'll hate me forever now, I thought.

Mama made a move toward the steps and I grabbed her. "No, Mama, you mustn't," I said. "Mrs. Manning can take care of Lillian. You need to come back to bed."

She struggled against my grasp, but was too weak to pull away and at last sagged against me and let me lead her back into the house. I settled her in a chair in the living room, ran to get a blanket from the linen closet, and took it to Mrs. Manning. Lillian was now lying on her back, moaning with the pain of her arm, which was obviously broken.

"She was lucky," said Mrs. Manning as she tucked the blanket around Lillian. "That tree branch broke her fall. She'll be all right, I think, but we'd better call the doctor. Can you stay with her while I make the call?"

I nodded and looked at her with tears in my eyes.

Mrs. Manning put an arm around me. "It's going to be all right, dear," she said, and then went into the house to make the call.

I sat there next to Lillian, listening to her moan, watching her lips quiver, and felt an overwhelming love for this little sister whom I'd resented for so long.

"I'm so sorry," I said. "I should have taken better care of you."

Lillian stopped moaning and looked up at me with her clear blue eyes. "I should have let you," she said, then closed her eyes again and was quiet.

Mrs. Manning came back. I've called the doctor and put your mother back to bed and given her one of her pills to settle her down," she said. "She'd like to see you, Marcia."

Fear struck me again as I thought of what Mama might say, and I hesitated.

"Go ahead, dear," Mrs. Manning urged gently.

I leaned over and kissed Lillian on the forehead, then rose and walked up the steps and into the house. Mama's makeshift bedroom, which had once been Papa's study, was dimly lit from the curtained windows, but I could see her lying against her pillows. I thought at first that she was asleep, but then she opened her eyes, smiled softly at me and held out her hand toward me. I took it and sat down on the edge of her bed.

"Lillian was a naughty girl to climb up on the roof that way," she said.

I nodded. After a few seconds, I said, "Mama, I really do try to look after her, but–"

"I know you do, dear, but I know, too, that you sometimes get to daydreaming and don't notice what she's up to."

I nodded and looked away, knowing that what she said was true.

"But I also know that Lillian takes advantage of you and doesn't mind what you say," Mama continued. "I'm going to have a talk with your father about that."

I turned my eyes back to look into hers. "Oh, Mama," I said, "if you only would."

She smiled and squeezed my hand and after a minute or two of silence, I knew she had fallen asleep.

Meanwhile, the doctor had come. He and Mrs. Manning brought Lillian into the house. They took her to the kitchen, where he set her arm and put a cast on it. He looked her over and said she didn't seem to have any other serious injuries, but recommended a couple of days in bed. "I'll be by to see her tomorrow," he promised as he left.

Lillian and I talked a lot during the next few days. She confided her dreams of becoming a ballerina and her discouragement at the interruption in her training. I told her of mine to become a writer. We encouraged each other and spoke of our worries about Mama and our guilty feelings about needing more attention from her and from Daddy.

Poor Mama didn't live long after that, and in the years that followed, with housekeepers and relatives coming in to look after things, the three of us clustered protectively against them. Even so, the triangulation among us continued. Lillian and I grew in our closeness and tended to exclude Billy – or Bill, as he demanded to be called now – but both of us vied for Bill's attention and friendship, so each of us felt left out from time to time. Bill represented a kind of steady authority that neither Daddy nor the various temporary mother figures in the household could offer. Thus, even now, sixty years later, and having married and raised families of our own, we each keep a lovingly wary eye on who's getting more attention from whom. It's kept us interested.

IN DEEP WOODS
Based on: Smoky, Latch, Apathy, Unlike

Unlike my previous visits to this woodsy spot on Claghorn Creek, this cozy little log cabin with its smoky fireplace, I had failed to latch onto the joy of its quiet comfort and felt only a leaden apathy.

My first impulse was to blame it on being here alone – without Ben. Although I'd been here alone many times in the past, this was different. This was the first time I'd been here since my husband had left. There was no Ben to go home to. I could stay here forever, for all anyone would care. I could paint every wildflower, every pond, every arching branch for as many miles around me as I could walk. It had often seemed to me as though that would be an ideal life for me. With all that freedom, I could make the name Mary Tiller on a painting really mean something. Now, however, I simply sat slumped in a faded chintz-covered armchair like a tired old pillow and stared into the black depths of the river rock fireplace.

Apathy. Yes, that was the word for the way I felt – or did not feel. It was an emptiness. A blankness. Damn Ben. Why couldn't he have at least given me cause for anger when he left? He'd been so reasonable. So fair about money and property and all. More than fair, if truth be told, and when my friend Linda had tried to cheer me by recounting my material assets, I felt a shower of guilt.

"Why should I have all this?" I asked her. A pleasant condo with a view of Mt. Hood and the Willamette River. This cabin, which had always been my favorite retreat. A good, reliable two-year-old car. Enough income to allow me to live comfortably – even somewhat lavishly if I could start selling my paintings. "What have I really done to earn it?"

"You were a good homemaker. A good mother. A good wife for 35 years," said Linda. "Ben would never have been as successful as he was without you."

I mused over that for a minute or two while I peeled an avocado for the salad I was making for our lunch. Good homemaker? Yes, I took pride in my pretty, well-kept house and imaginative, healthful meals, even back in the days of a scant budget. Good mother? I think so, though I fear my children would not fully agree with that assessment. But good wife? I'd gone through the motions, certainly. I'd been agreeable most of the time, but … "apathetic," I said aloud, and Linda looked at me with surprise.

"Apathetic?" she repeated. "How can you say that? You've kept your life so full! Your family, your friends, the church, your community, your painting. You can't be apathetic and do all that."

I smiled then, arranging avocado and tomato wedges around mounds of shrimp salad. Although her accolade had not really reached the place where I was hurting, I didn't want to try to sort it out now and spoil our lunch, so I said, "Thanks, Linda. You always know how to make me feel better."

But now, here I was at the cabin with that word plaguing me again, and no Linda to brush it away for me. I didn't want to be this way. I didn't want to live this way. Again and again in my life I'd tried to generate passion. Enthusiasm. I'd smiled, talked, listened, volunteered, and acted my part so well that even my best friend didn't know. But Ben knew and he'd finally given up and found someone who could really love him. The children knew, and had gone on into their own lives, leaving me behind.

Now, here I was alone. No responsibilities. No one to need

anything from me. No one but myself to put on an act for. Tears welled in my eyes and spilled over, streaming down my cheeks and off my chin. I needed a tissue and got up and stumbled into the bathroom. I blew my nose and then, as I stood there dabbing at my eyes, the mirror reflected a plaque that had hung on that opposite wall for years.

Be careful what you wish for, you might get it.

I laughed, and blew my nose again and dabbed at my eyes some more. I read the plaque again, and laughed some more. I put some fresh tissues in my pocket, for I knew there would be more tears, but I left the bathroom, walked through the shadowy great-room, past the cold, smoky black fireplace, and out onto the porch. I inhaled the soft, fresh, sun-shot air of the surrounding forest. A squirrel scampered up a tree and startled a bluejay into flight. The creek sang to me in an almost intelligible babble, and a gentle breeze lifted a nearby fir branch as though in greeting. My recovery had begun.

A LUCKY BRAKE
Based on: Poppy, Pudgy, Double, Valise

As I braked my car for a stop signal, I glanced out of the window at a pudgy girl sitting on a valise, munching a large poppy seed bagel, and did a double-take. I was almost sure she was the daughter of a woman I knew back home in Springdale.

The light turned green before I could think what, if anything, I should do about this, but as I drove on, the impression I had of her bothered me more and more. I'm not the kind of person to impose on another's privacy, and this girl, even if she was who I thought she was, was a virtual stranger. Nevertheless, I turned right at the next corner and drove around the block, almost hoping her bus would have come by the time I could get back there, and she would be gone.

She was still there, however, and as I stopped beside her I opened the window on the passenger side of my car, unlocked the door, and called to her.

"Are you Allison Blair?" I asked.

The girl looked startled and got to her feet as though to run.

"It's all right," I said, sure now, that it was she. "I'm Nancy Park from Springdale. I know your mother. I just wondered if you'd like a ride somewhere."

The girl hesitated and eyed me suspiciously.

"Come on, Allison," I said. "If you change your mind I'll let you out at the next bus stop."

She climbed in and held her valise on her lap.

"You can put that in back if you like," I said.

She gave me a sidewise glance and said, "No, I'd rather hold it."

There was nothing obvious about her to arouse my concern. She wore lived-in jeans and a rather soiled navy nylon jacket, but she looked fairly clean and well fed, and her long, straight blonde hair was pulled back and more or less held by a red rubber band. She was only about twelve, though, and so young to be alone, 300 miles from home, and her wariness told me this was no ordinary vacation.

"Where were you intending to go?" I asked.

"I wanted to get out to the highway and hitch a ride east," she said.

"And then what?" I asked.

She was silent. I made a decision.

"Tell you what," I said. "I'm living here now, and have a hide-a-bed in my den. If you'll call your mom and let her know you're okay, you can stay with me till you get things straightened out."

Allison looked at me warily for several seconds before she answered. "How do I know I can trust you," she asked at last.

"Trust me in what way, Allison? I won't hurt you, certainly."

"You'll tell my mom where I am and she'll make me go home."

"We'll have to let her know you're with me and get her permission for you to stay," I said. "That's the law."

"But...." she started, then stopped.

"We'll talk to her, Allison. She'll be so glad to know you're safe that she'll agree to almost anything. I promise."

"How do you know?"

"I don't know her well, but I know she loves you and tries to be a good mother to you."

"But she's getting married again."

"So?" I asked.

"He looks at me funny," she said.

Shocked, it took me a minute to let this sink in and think how to respond, but then said, "So you've run away. Does that make you feel safer?"

When she didn't answer, I went on. "Allison, you need to talk with your mother about this. Running away won't solve the problem."

She remained silent, looking out of the car window. "I don't know this part of town," she said. "Are you taking me to your place now?"

"Is that okay?" I asked.

"Will you let me go if I don't want to stay?"

"Of course," I said, "but I'll try to arrange for somewhere you can go and be safe."

She thought about this and nodded.

We got to my apartment and called her mother. I stepped out of the room and closed the door. It was a long conversation. When she came out of the room there were tears in her eyes and on her cheeks and chin, but she was smiling.

"Mom's coming to get me," she said. "She'll be here tomorrow.

I smiled, relieved that my intervention had brought this result, that Allison was not, now, hitch-hiking into possible disaster. My stop for that red light was a lucky "brake" for us both, I reflected.

ANNIVERSARY SUNDAY
Based on: Malady, Wallop, Hymnal, Impair

Aubrey Bains worried that the nature of his malady would impair his ability to wallop his congregation with a rousing sermon to mark his fiftieth year as its pastor until it dawned on him to let his hymnal do it for him.

For months now, the aging minister had had increasing difficulty with his voice, which no doctor had been able to diagnose. That fact, almost as much as the problem itself, troubled him. He wondered if it was God's way of telling him to step aside in favor of his young assistant. Indeed, since the failure of Aubrey's once resonant voice had begun to plague him, 35-year-old David Quince had done an excellent job filling in for him. He had fired the old man's vision with his youthful style and the congregation had responded with enthusiasm. Now, more and more, David had led their collaboration into channels that had never occurred to Aubrey. Maybe Anniversary Sunday's service should be his swan song. Maybe the old guy wasn't needed any longer.

Aubrey lifted the hymnal from among the books on his desk and opened it at random. Let my congregation sing a farewell service to me, he thought. I will choose my favorite hymns, they will sing them. I will stand, smile my gratitude, and drape my own stole over David's shoulders.

David listened with quiet, respectful understanding as Aubrey, firmly and bravely, presented his proposal to him as they sat together in Aubrey's study that afternoon. He knew what it had

81

cost the old man to make it. "It won't be a retirement ceremony, Aubrey," he said, "but a graduation ceremony – for both of us. I will fill the pulpit, but your experience, wisdom, and spirit will continue to guide all of us. You'll have more time for the personal contact that you love. You can help me to grow stronger in the roles you've played all these years."

The old man smiled fondly at the young minister. "You've already proven your abilities, David," he said. "I'm afraid my pride has not let me use them as fully as I should have. It seems that God has seen fit to remedy that."

"Time has never brought me a change I was ready for," said David. "I think it's that way for all of us."

Aubrey rose and stepped to one side of the big, cluttered mahogany desk that the women of the church had tried in vain to dust from time to time over the years. He gestured toward the black leather-upholstered wing chair he'd just vacated. "Go ahead, son," he said. "Try it on for size."

David paused, looking at the chair and then at Aubrey. "I don't think it'd fit," he said. "My own office will be more comfortable for me, and for the parishioners who will visit me there as well."

Aubrey returned the young minister's warm gaze, thinking how wrong David was about the fit, but accepted his decision with silent gratitude. "Harrumph," he said, clearing his throat and reaching for his hymnal. "Well, do borrow this," he said, handing the book to David. "I've marked all my favorite hymns in there, and expect to hear them all on my big Fiftieth Anniversary Sunday."

"And so you shall," said David, riffling through the small forest of bookmarks, and then offering Aubrey his hand. "I'll give this to the choir director immediately."

"No, no," Aubrey objected. "Not the choir director, just the organist. This is a job for the entire congregation."

David laughed gently. "You're right, of course," he said. "It will be grand. The congregation will love it."

The two men shook hands, then, and David left the old pastor alone. Aubrey resumed his seat and looked around this walnut-panelled study. There were comfortable chairs, cherished books, paintings of a sunrise over the ocean, of a tumbling stream in a forest glade, and a favorite quotation from Joseph Addison had been calligraphed by a friend and set into a black wooden frame:

The grand essentials to happiness in this life are something to do, something to love and something to hope for.

I have all of those," he reflected, and smiling comfortably, he leaned back into his chair and worried no more about his own future, that of the congregation, or about his Anniversary Sunday.

SMALL-TOWN JUSTICE
Based on: Hunter, Nutria, Empire, Pilfer

The capture of a dark, scruffy-looking man claiming to be a nutria hunter who was caught trying to pilfer a packet of secret documents from a remote, snow-bound Alaskan outpost caused an immediate outcry that here was a spy from an evil empire.

The man carried no papers of his own; only a shotgun and a few rounds of ammunition. Moreover, he seemed to be suffering from amnesia, unable to remember his name or where he'd come from. He spoke English with a cultivated English accent, and apparently no other language.

On interrogation, he said he'd been lost, separated from his hunting party, and that he was merely seeking maps or some means of locating himself. He said that he had at first thought the garrison to be deserted, and was relieved when the men returned, even though it was to arrest him, for he was quite unprepared to deal with his situation and needed help. His captors believed none of this, of course. In the first place, they sniggered, nutria are not found in Alaska, but in South America. Secondly, one would not be hunting nutria with a shotgun, but setting traps for them. They had some doubts about his amnesia, yet considering his story on the whole, thought that he was either an inventive fake, or that he really did have something seriously wrong with his brain. In short order, a helicopter came to take him away to a military base near Tacoma, Washington, where he was imprisoned.

Meanwhile, Amelia Thornton sat at home awaiting the return

of her husband, Ted, from an Alaskan hunting trip he'd won in a lottery. He had not been expected home for another week, but when she read the accounts of the suspected spy in the newspapers, and saw glimpses of him on television, she began to worry.

Truly, the bearded, dishevelled person she saw did not closely resemble Ted, though perhaps her heart would not admit that he did. Nor did she recognize his voice, which was so hoarse as to be barely audible. Nevertheless, she called the telephone number shown on the brochure from Alaskan Adventures, the company who had offered the trip as a promotional lottery prize. The woman she spoke with there was polite and tried to be reassuring, but was of little help. She had information about the organization and departure of the expedition, but nothing current. She promised to try to make contact and call back, but when hours passed and Amelia had heard nothing, she began to worry in earnest.

Now, the Thorntons were a quiet, middle-class, middle-aged couple who had come from northern England a little more than a year before. Ted was branch manager of the bank in the small town of Pine Valley, Oregon, in which they lived. She worked as a secretary in a real estate office there. Their three children were grown and scattered hither and yon, none of them in the United States. In the thirty years she and Ted had been married, she had never known him to take an interest in hunting, and she was surprised when he accepted the prize offered on the telephone. Somehow, however, the idea of going hunting in Alaska sounded exciting to him, and exactly the kind of thing that would perk up his rather drab life. Inasmuch as Alaskan Adventures had promised to take care of all details of the trip, including clothing and equipment, Ted had not concerned himself with them, though they both had the idea that he would be hunting elk. No one had ever said anything about nutria.

The claim by the man in custody that he was suffering from

amnesia sounded an alarm bell in Amelia's mind, however, causing her to suspect that he might be her husband. Ted had had occasional temporary departures of memory in the past. Extreme stress seemed to trigger them in him. If, indeed, he had been abandoned in the wilds of Alaska without identification or provision, the stress assailing him would no doubt be extreme to the utmost. This nutria business could be just a part of his dementia.

Oh, she thought, if only Alaskan Adventures would call and tell her the expedition was on track! If only – but this was unreasonable – Ted would call or, better still, come home!

Amelia and Ted had made a number of casual friends in their new little community, but no one close. Now Amelia searched her mind for someone she could turn to. Someone she could talk to about this bizarre situation without the danger of gossip spreading throughout this tightly knit little town and endangering not only their social status, but perhaps even Ted's job. Perhaps she should call the newspaper, she thought now. Surely the writer of the newspaper account of the spy story could put her in touch with someone who could give her answers. But there again was the danger of putting herself and Ted in the limelight. It was impossible to know where that would lead, and she still was not entirely convinced that the man she'd seen on television was Ted.

She spent the night watching CNN, waiting for more news, for more pictures of the alleged spy, but they kept repeating the same bits of information, showing the same video clips. She listened, nevertheless, trying to divine something definite that would either identify this man as her husband or prove that it was not he. By morning, she had made up her mind. The only thing to do was to call the FBI, to go to where the man was imprisoned, and see for herself whether it was Ted or not. If it was, her place was by his side; if it was not – oh, what a relief that would be.

Within two hours, Amelia was in her car, headed for Tacoma, where she would be met and escorted. She drove as fast as she dared, met the FBI agent as planned, endured questioning, was at last was brought into the presence of the mysterious nutria hunter, and threw her arms around her husband.

Within moments, Ted remembered who he was; remembered how he had ventured, clothed, but carrying nothing more than the shot- gun with which to protect himself from wild animals as he made a midnight trip to the privy. He remembered how he had apparently taken a wrong turn on the way back and had become lost; how he had found the unguarded military garrison, had, in desperation, broken a window to gain entry, and minutes later been apprehended.

Now, news bulletins rang out across the country: The identity of the "Alaskan Nutria Hunter" had been established; his name was Theodore James Thornton. He was a bank manager in Pine Valley, Oregon. Whether or not the authorities believed his story, the people of Pine Valley put him on trial over coffee cups and bridge games. They glued themselves to their television sets, and their telephone lines were alive with gossip. The consensus was that while the Thorntons seemed nice enough, no one really knew them; they were so British; they were so private, so aloof. Ted Thornton could very well be a spy.

Within a few days, Ted was released on bail, pending trial. He and Amelia came home to Pine Valley, but it was to a chilly, suspicious welcome. When at last he was exonerated, the town's people reached out to them in embarrassment, tried to make amends. A number of people called to apologize for their lack of support, but it was too late. Ted and Amelia tried to forgive them. Ted even went so far as to quip that if the town could forgive him for going nutria hunting in Alaska with a shotgun, he could forgive the town for convicting him without a trial. It was soon clear, however, that the Thorntons and the people of Pine Valley would never really learn to trust one another; no relationship could ever grow.

Within a month, Ted was able to arrange a transfer into

Eugene, and the Thorntons began the process of moving and settling into this larger, more sophisticated city. As for the fabric of society in Pine Valley, the damage was soon mended. The few people who voiced mild criticism of the town's prejudice were soon quieted by the sheer comfort of belonging.

OF BREAD AND DREAMS
Based on: Focus, Flour, Muscle, Ponder

Have you ever stopped to ponder the fact that as one places one's focus on the flour and muscle involved in making bread, one's problems often seem to solve themselves? Oh yes, of course the same thing can happen with almost any physical activity, but for Myrtle, there was nothing quite like making bread.

One morning last week, for instance, Myrtle rose bleary-eyed after a sleepless night. You see, her daughter Marilyn was marrying a young man from a socially prominent family and the wedding plans were growing far beyond Myrtle's dreams, not to mention her husband's financial resources. Hundreds of guests were to be invited. A large, beautiful church had been booked, a fashionable restaurant for the reception reserved, and two bands hired for listening during dinner, and dancing afterward. Marilyn would need a spectacular gown. She, herself would need something really special to wear. Her husband would need a tuxedo. Then there would be invitations and flowers and a photographer.

The list grew in Myrtle's mind. Marilyn was beside herself with excitement and neither Myrtle nor her husband could bear to broach their financial concerns. How could they? They had never denied Marilyn anything important to her, and this surely seemed to her the most important thing she had ever asked of them. To pay these bills would put them into debt for the rest of their lives. It would mean that they must enter their retirement years in seriously diminished circumstances. It was neither fair, reasonable, nor really responsible of them to accept this imposition. Still, how could they throw cold water on Marilyn's dreams? How could they reveal to the groom's family that they could not afford this kind of wedding?

Myrtle tied a clean white apron around her ample waist and pulled flour and butter and yeast from their places in her bright, airy kitchen. She measured and mixed till she had a shining ball of dough, which she kneaded briefly before setting it to rise beneath a blue and white tea towel in her big yellow earthenware bowl.

She tidied the kitchen, picked up the family room, put a load of laundry into the washer, watered her African violets, her mind still grinding away at her problem. At last, she checked the time and lifted the cloth to find her bread dough twice its size, ready for punching down and serious kneading.

She sprinkled flour on her pastry board, dumped the dough onto it, and plunged into her work. This was the part she loved. This was where she found her release. Her arms, hands, shoulders worked with rhythmic power, squeezing, pressing, turning, pausing to sprinkle more flour. Again and again, she repeated this routine until the task was complete and she began to form the elastic dough into loaves and rolls, place them in their pans, cover them, and set them to rise again.

Her energy was spent, and so, magically, was her anxiety. She washed her hands, took off her apron, and poured a cup of coffee. Myrtle didn't know where her mind had gone during that last half hour of the bread-making process, but it had come back with the realization that she and George were in charge here. It was for them to talk, to decide what contribution they would make, tell Marilyn, and let her take it from there. It was not the solution she would have liked, but it was responsible, it was fair, and it was necessary. She rocked back in her recliner, sipped her coffee, and enjoyed the aroma of rising bread.

COLUMBIA
Based on: Falter, Crayon, Jagged, Stigma

"There are plenty of people who falter in their lives, failing to attain their dreams, failing to overcome the stigma of poverty," said Columbia as she picked up a broken, jagged pastel crayon to trace a strong, bright red arc on her art pad, "but I'm not going to be one of them."

Columbia was not her original name. It is a name she adopted at a low point in her life, as she stood on the banks of that mighty river, and from that day onward it was all she ever used. This moment marked the end of a life for her, and the beginning of a new one. It was her Easter; her resurrection.

The early years of her former life had not really been all that bad. Yes, her family had been dirt poor. Her father drank up what little they had, but he was a peaceful, contented kind of drunk who never raised a hand against anyone. He just lazed around the house in his tattered, seldom washed jeans and undershirt, sipping warm beer and dozing, eating whatever was placed before him. Her mother cleaned other people's houses and watched their kids, taking little Thelma Jean, as she was known then, and her brother Tim with her till they were old enough to stay on their own.

It wasn't a bad life, just sad, and from the time Thelma was ten or eleven, she dreamed of escape. She dreamed of living in the kinds of houses her mother cleaned. She dreamed of having dancing lessons and wearing pretty clothes. She found other kids who shared those dreams, most of them looking up out of holes deeper than her own, and who hid out, avoiding the violence of their homes. And they learned to use drugs to escape to a better world. And they stole whatever they could for the money to finance those trips.

Thelma Jean was fifteen when she and her seventeen-year-old boyfriend, Joe, managed to buy an old car and take off across the country.

"This is our escape," she told Joe. "No more drugs, no more stealing. We're going to live decent or it's no use our going away."

Joe agreed, and they both tried. They settled in a small town, got a room in a cheap motel. Joe got a job in a gas station. She was too young to get a social security card, but she helped out at the motel and the owner paid her under the table.

They tried, but the pull of old habits was hard to resist. Joe bought some pot from a guy at the station and they shared it.

"This is not so bad," they told each other. "We can handle this." But then Joe brought home some coke and then some heroin. Joe stole money from the gas station and was fired. They moved on. They tried again, but this time it was hard for Joe to get a job because of his bad reference. They stayed off drugs for a while, but when opportunity came knocking, they couldn't resist answering the door.

Thelma Jean got pregnant. Joe left her a note on the bureau: "I'm sorry, honey, I just can't." She never saw him again. He died of an overdose a few days later.

Thelma Jean went to ask about an abortion, but was waylaid outside the clinic by some Right-to-Life people. They showed her pictures of fetuses at various stages. They told her how wrong it was to end this little innocent life. They told her God would give her the strength if only she would do the right thing. "Don't worry," they said. "All will be well."

She bought it all. She went back to the room she'd shared with Joe. She flushed all the dope down the john. She thought of her own mother and how hard she'd worked. "What if Mama had aborted me?" she asked herself. "I wouldn't even be here." Then she looked in the mirror and began to cry. "Maybe it would have been a good thing."

Months passed. Thelma Jean worked as a waitress and stayed away from drugs. She saved every penny she could and began to feel hopeful that she could cope. The baby, a girl, was born in a welfare clinic. She went back to her room and bedded the baby in a cardboard box held by two folding chairs. She got into bed, exhausted, and slept. The baby cried. She nursed her and went back to sleep.

A week passed with Thelma Jean eating, sleeping, nursing, changing diapers, bathing little Chloe in the bathroom sink – and worrying. Her small stash of bills was dwindling. God would provide the strength, those people had said. But who would pay for groceries and diapers? How could she work? How could she do it all when she was so tired? So very tired.

Another week passed. Thelma Jean had applied for welfare in order to get medical care. Now she needed child care. She needed money. She needed so much. She thought of her mother again, of her mother's life, of her own life and the hopelessness of it. She looked at Chloe, so small, so trusting. She wanted something better than this for her child. Something better than she could ever give her. She wanted to break this cycle of poverty, of neediness.

Late that night, Thelma Jean bathed Chloe and dressed her in a pink bunny suit she'd picked up at a rummage sale before Chloe was even born. She tied a pink ribbon in her fine, curly brown hair. She kissed her, laid her in her box, and covered her warmly. She put the box in the car along with some clothing for herself and a bag of art supplies she'd been dragging around with her for years. She drove a hundred miles, into a large city. She parked in the parking lot of a hospital and took the box inside. She took the elevator to the third floor. There was no one in sight. She set the box on the floor, stepped back into the elevator and pressed the lobby button. The door closed. When it opened again, Thelma Jean crossed the lobby, walked out to her car, and drove away, confident that Chloe would find love and care and the kind of life that she couldn't give her.

She drove on, another hundred miles or so, and came to a shabby motel. She rented a room. She had a few sleeping pills that she'd swiped from the clinic. She took four. At about two the next afternoon, she was awakened by a pounding at her door. It was the motel owner, wanting her out or to pay for another night.

She felt groggy, but showered, washed her hair and dressed in clean jeans and a clean blue work shirt that Joe had left behind. She got into her car and drove until she reached the Columbia River. At a view point, she got out of her car and stretched.

The Columbia River, she mused, standing on its bank and watching the strong current that seemed to flow through her very soul. She perched, then, on the fender of her car, contemplating that flow, allowing it to cleanse her mind, allowing it to bring the realization of what she'd done in abandoning her baby. Tears came. Wracking sobs came. And then rational thought. I'll go back and face the music. I'll arrange for Chloe's adoption. I'll start a new life for myself.

It was then that she pulled the bedraggled pad of drawing paper and a sack of odd, broken pastel crayons from the trunk of her car and made her first mark, the strong, bright red arc across the page. "Columbia!" she exclaimed. "My name is Columbia! I'm not going to be one of them! I am Columbia!"

A LESSON IN BALANCE
Based on: Agile, Itchy, Bewail, Enmity

"Ladies," said Angela Conroy to her class of eleven-year-old ballet students, "you can stand around and bewail your itchy, cumbersome costumes, and spark enmity at me for making you wear them, or you can learn to be agile and adorable in them and make your audience love you. The choice is yours."

She turned away from them, to fiddle with the tape player and find the part of Mussorgsky's "Pictures at an Exhibition" that called for these befeathered baby chicks. It was not that Angela was not empathetic with the girls' complaints. Many were the times that she – as student and as professional dancer – had had to wear costumes that seemed designed to thwart her agility and grace. She, too, had been prone to complain, but learned to accept such costumes as part of her challenge as a dancer.

"Places, please, ladies," she said, turning to face them again. "You know the routine."

She pressed the button to start the music. "Ready, now begin," she said, and watched as the girls struggled sullenly through the routine they'd learned in simple tights and leotards. Now, they found their timing off and their movements impeded by their costumes.

Angela stopped the music. "Perhaps what you need to do," she said, "is to take some time to get acquainted with these costumes. Look at yourselves in the mirror as you practice the moves you need to make. They will feel different to you in these costumes, but you can learn to adjust."

The girls found places in front of the mirrored wall and watched themselves as they practiced their stiff-kneed gait, their stubby-winged flutter, the rapid, awkward bends from the hip. Soon, they were laughing at themselves and each other.

Angela watched for a few minutes, worried that she'd lost control of her class. She moved among them, correcting, demonstrating, directing their attention to the effects of various moves and attitudes. She believed it was her job to be serious, to maintain discipline, and so stifled her own laughter, her own sense of fun.

At last, she clapped her hands sharply for attention and the girls stopped their giggling and looked at her, trying vainly for the solemnity they had learned their teacher expected of them.

"I think we've been silly for quite long enough, ladies. Please take your places for the dance."

Angela restarted the music and the girls began their routine, but all the life had gone out of them. They were no longer the funny, adorable chicks they'd been a minute before, but appeared wooden. Mechanical.

Angela interrupted the music. The girls looked at her. "Your timing is better, ladies," she said, "but you're not feeling the music. You have no spirit. Try to capture the way you felt when you were giggling in front of the mirror a few minutes ago."

"But Miss Conroy," said one of the girls. "We were just being silly then. Now we're dancing."

It took Angela a beat or two to grasp the truth in the girl's words, but then it was as though a light had come into her mind. She had been so concerned with discipline and control that she had, herself, dismissed the fun of Mussorgsky's music and taken it away from her students.

"You're right," she said with a smile. "You were just being silly before. You were acting like silly little baby chicks. You were having fun. Mussorgsky would have loved you. Now try having fun with his music and my choreography."

Restarting the music, Angela turned once more to the girls and, still smiling, said, "Okay now, places again, girls." She felt self-consciously aware of this unprecedented informality, and at the same time, an almost palpable response from the girls. It frightened her a little, and yet, as she watched the girls gradually relax and respond more spontaneously to the music, the execution of her choreography so much more as she had pictured it, she began, herself, to relax.

The routine ended. Angela clapped her hands, laughing with delight, and so did the girls. She walked among them, praising each one, yet making suggestions for improvement. The girls smiled and nodded, trying out the new moves.

The chiming of a clock signaled the end of the lesson period. The girls held their places, looking expectantly at their teacher for dismissal. Angela, hands on her hips, took a final appraising look at them before she said, "That's all for today, girls. I'm proud of you."

The girls filed into the dressing room, removed their now less onerous costumes, hung them carefully, and dressed in their street clothes. Each smiled shyly and said good-bye to Angela as they left the studio.

The girls learned a valuable lesson in balance today, thought Angela as she watched them go, and so did I.

SLEIGHT OF HEART
Based on: Fuzzy, Prune, Abrupt, Tuxedo

With an abrupt stoke of his wand, the tall dark man wearing an elaborate turban and a gold satin tuxedo transformed a wrinkled old prune into a plump, fuzzy toy rabbit. The audience, composed mostly of children, laughed, and clapped its hands in delight.

"How did he do that?" everyone wondered, but of course they were never to know for, after the show, they filed out of the theater into the soft summer evening air to pursue their own lives, giving scant further thought to this performer and his tricks.

The magician watched them go, collected his fee for his performance, packed his gear, and drove off into the night in his nondescript minivan. He made it a practice never to stay overnight in a town in which he had performed, lest he meet some of the members of his audience and thus lose some of his mystique.

When he came upon a modest motel along the highway, he stopped and, having removed his tuxedo, his turban, and his dramatic eyebrows, engaged a room for the night. Alone in his room, he removed the rest of his makeup and looked at himself in the mirror with sad eyes.

The youthful, glamorous man was no more. Before him was mirrored a drab, aging man who had grown tired of keeping up the pretense of turning himself into an enchanting fake; of transforming an ordinary old prune into a charming toy, all for the entertainment of people who neither knew nor cared about the man behind the sham.

There came an urgent knock at his door. Startled at first, he opened it to find a bedraggled little girl in tears who burst in upon him and hugged him around his knees.

His first instinct was to back away, to free himself from this small intruder, but something held him. Instead, he clasped her curly head tenderly between his hands and looked deeply into her liquid eyes.

"Whatever is the matter?" he asked, but she merely sobbed and buried her face in his thigh and said nothing.

In another instant, a large man appeared and grabbed him by the shirt front.

"What are you doing with this child?" the man shouted.

Wrenching himself away from both, he shoved them roughly outside and slammed the door. He heard the little girl cry out briefly before she was silenced. He cowered, frightened in his room and poured himself a tumbler of Bourbon, and then another. Eventually he fell into a stupor across his bed. When he woke in the middle of the next morning, he remembered vaguely that.... No, he didn't want to remember that.

He got himself a cup of coffee from the motel office, watched television for a while, then showered, dressed and went on his way.

The magician had no gig that night so, after eating his lonely dinner in a cheap diner, he bought a newspaper to take back to his hotel room. There, on the front page, was a picture of the little girl from last night's episode. She was missing. Her mother was frantic. There was a reward for information.

He read the article a second time and stared at the picture. No, he thought, this is none of my business. I don't want to get mixed up in it. He turned to other pages of the paper, scanned other headlines, tried to put the little girl out of his mind, but could not. Even as he looked at other pictures, her image was before him. Not the smiling face of the newspaper photo, but the tearful, terrified face he'd seen the night before.

There was no phone in his room. He would have to use the one in the hall. No, he thought again. I don't really know anything useful anyway. Others must have seen them. Surely someone else will call.

He lay down on the bed and stared at the water-stained ceiling of his room. He couldn't rest. He turned on the television, but couldn't focus on the sit-com in progress. The program ended. There were commercials. There was a news break. The little girl's mother appeared, tearfully appealing to anyone who'd seen … anyone who knew anything at all … please call the police. Please, just dial 911."

As though levitated by some unseen force, the magician put his feet on the floor and felt in his pocket for change. He rose and walked to the door of his room, opened it, and stepped out into the hallway. The phone was at the far end. He walked there as in a dream, dropped coins into the slot, and dialed. He asked for the police.

"My name is John Howard," he said. "Last night I was in my room … a little girl came and … a large man came and … yes, I believe I could identify him."

It was almost midnight when John Howard stabbed his finger at an image in the police mug book. "That's the man," he said. "Yes, I'm sure."

Within a few days the man was apprehended. The little girl was rescued. The grateful mother invited John Howard to dinner. He accepted and afterward entertained them by turning a prune into a rabbit, which he presented to the little girl.

"I might have known you were a magician," said the mother. "You made my daughter reappear."

John Howard laughed gently, beaming with pride and pleasure. As he sat there, then, drinking coffee and chatting with this woman and her child, he knew that an even more amazing transformation had taken place in his own heart. He knew it would change his life forever.

HOME IS WHERE THE HEARTH IS
Based on: Newly, Flame, Woeful, Levity

A newly kindled flame in the ancient fieldstone fireplace introduced a glimmer of levity to the woeful atmosphere of the long neglected old house. Allison Babcock stood hugging herself as she gazed glumly at the rainwater dripping copiously from the porch eves beyond the grimy picture windows of the living room.

"Come on, honey," coaxed her husband, Ted, as he swiped at cobwebs with a scraggly old broom. "With a little spit and polish, this place can be our salvation."

Salvation was indeed what this inheritance had seemed when the destitute couple had read of it in a letter from the executor of Ted's great-aunt Maude's estate. The old lady had died months ago in a nursing home, and it had been difficult to locate the itinerant Babcocks.

You see, Ted was a barely surviving freelance writer and photographer, Allie a ceramist with about the same degree of financial success. Both had worked from their small rented home in the outskirts of Forest Grove, Oregon. An electrical short had caused a fire that destroyed everything they had except their ten-year-old station wagon, the clothes they wore, and about $500.00 in the bank. Since then, they had bunked with various friends and worked at whatever they could find to get a new start.

Allie wiped a tear from her eye and smiled faintly as she turned to see Ted's violent attempts to battle the dankness that surrounded them. He reminded her of Don Quixote.

Noticing this small brightening of her attitude, Ted paused in his efforts, put an arm around her shoulders, and walked her over to the fireplace. "There's my girl," he said as she extended her hands toward the growing blaze. He dusted off a low wooden stool and set it for her to sit on.

"You just sit here and get warm while I run out and try to get us some water and electricity turned on," he said.

"Okay," she said, squeezing his hand. "Bring us back a cup of coffee, will you?"

"Will do," he promised. "It's apt to be a while before the utility guys can get here. Coffee will help." He kissed the top of her head and left.

Allie sat there for a while, letting the fire warm and cheer her, then got up and began wandering through the house, appraising its possibilities.

The carpets, curtains, and upholstered furniture were hopelessly lost to accumulated dust and moisture. The beds had become squirrel nests. Wooden furniture – tables, chairs, bureaus – could be salvaged with a little work. The dining chairs would need new pads, but she could do that. Peeling wallpaper needed replacement and the kitchen needed new paint and new hinges on the cabinet doors. That would take not only work, but money, she reflected. The stove and refrigerator dated from the 50s, perhaps, but they looked okay and someone had taken the refrigerator door off its hinges. Iron skillets and a Dutch oven needed scouring and recuring, but otherwise the cooking utensils weren't bad. The silver plated flatware needed polish, but it was of a simple, classic pattern that she liked. She didn't think much of the Desert Rose pattern dishes, but they'd do. And there was an assortment of glassware. Aunt Maude evidently liked glass. Someone had wisely removed all of the leftover food stuffs from the cupboards, yet, oddly, there was wine. A dozen or so bottles, mostly red, lay cradled in a built-in wine rack.

Allie had not known Aunt Maude when she lived here, but was wishing now that she could have. She wondered again at

Maude's having left this place to Ted, who'd paid her scant attention. She smiled wryly as she cast another glance around her. Had Maude meant it as a blessing or a curse?

A sound from outside the kitchen window drew Allie's attention and she looked out to see Ted and another man approaching the back of the house. She opened the door and stepped out onto the porch. The rain had now thinned to a fine mist.

"Hi there! I'm Tom," said the man in greeting. "Welcome to Nehalem. In about two shakes of a lamb's tail, you'll be electrified."

"I'm already electrified that you've come so quickly!" Allie enthused.

"Ted was just lucky. I happened to be in," said Tom, "and my old buddy Burt is in the front yard turning on the water."

Ted and Allie exchanged elated glances and then watched as Tom went about turning on their electricity and engaging the switches in their breaker box. "I'm glad you're here," he said, looking around at the fir trees and the neglected rhododendrons. This was a pretty nice old place when Maude lived here. It could be again."

Ted smiled and nodded agreement as Burt came around the corner of the house to join them.

"You'll think your plumbing is coming apart for a little while, but you're in business," he said after introductions had been made. He handed Ted a card. "Here's the name of a good plumber if you need one," he added.

The four of them stood there in the shelter of the porch overhang and exchanged pleasantries for a few minutes before Allie asked if the men would like to come in and get warm and dry by the fire.

"Oh, no thanks," said Tom, and Burt allowed that they'd better be getting back to work.

"What nice people," Allie said as she and Ted went back into the house.

Ted tried the kitchen light. It worked. Allie tried the faucet in the sink and they both laughed at the gurgling and banging and at the ragged sputter of brown water that spewed forth.

"We're going to be all right," said Ted, taking Allie into his arms.

"Yes, we are," she murmured into his neck, and when, after a minute or two, they wandered back into the living room, they found that their fire had settled into a quiet, steady, warming glow that had taken the damp chill out of the room. "I'm ready to make a home here now," Allie said, smiling softly into the fire.

"Well then, let's have at it," agreed Ted, and they went to work.

RUSE, RUSEE, AND RUSSO
Based on: Barium, Superb, Magnet, Pounce

Despite the justly deserved reputation as a social magnet earned by Margaret Manning's superb charm, Police Lieutenant Russo was inclined to pounce upon her as a suspect in the barium poisoning of her husband Gilbert.

The first thing Russo did, of course, was to have his men search the Manning home for the source of the poison. They didn't have far to look. A box of bicarbonate of soda found in the bathroom medicine cabinet was found to be liberally laced with barium salts of a particularly lethal variety.

When questioned, Margaret turned pale. "Yes," she admitted, "I did give Gilbert a dose of bicarb that night. We'd been out. He'd eaten a lot of rich food. He was suffering from indigestion."

"And when you learned at the hospital that your husband had died of barium poisoning, you certainly wouldn't suspect the soda, would you?" suggested Russo.

"Why no. Of course not. I myself have quite a lot of digestive trouble and bicarb is my favorite remedy. I took some from that very box only a night or two before."

"And was it a favorite remedy of your husband's as well?" asked Russo.

Margaret cast down her eyes and fidgeted with the damp handkerchief she held in her hands. "No, Lieutenant, it was not. His favored remedy was Alka Seltzer, but we didn't have any. We'd run out. I didn't want to tell him that because it would put him in a rage. I simply mixed some bicarb and he drank it without noticing the difference."

"And was your husband in the habit of getting into a rage over things, Mrs. Manning?"

"He had a quick temper, yes. He'd never hit me or anything like that, but he'd get very angry over any little inconvenience or disappointment. He expected me to be efficient in seeing to his needs. I did try, but...." and here Margaret broke off sobbing. "If only there'd been Alka Seltzer, I wouldn't have given him bicarb and...."

Russo sat quietly for a few moments as Margaret wept silently into her sodden handkerchief, and a new light dawned in his mind. If the husband didn't ordinarily use the soda – and the wife did – perhaps it was the wife who was the intended victim.

"Mrs. Manning," he said gently, "you've already told us that you could think of no one who would want to harm your husband." Margaret nodded and met the lieutenant's eyes with her own. "Is there anyone you can think of who, well, who would want you to die?" he went on.

Margaret's teary blue eyes grew large at this suggestion. "Not really," she said after a few moments' thought. "Although...." she added, but then she hesitated.

"Although?" Russo prompted.

"Oh, no," Margaret demurred. "Just a foolish thought."

"Foolish thoughts can sometimes be very valuable," said Russo.

Margaret spread her handkerchief across her lap, smoothing it with her hands, then folded it carefully. "Perhaps," she said at last, "but … let me think about this."

Russo rose from his chair. "You have my card," he said. "Call me if you have any ideas, foolish or otherwise."

"I will," she promised, smiling wanly as she rose to bid him good-bye.

Russo left feeling somewhat relieved that maybe, after all, he would not have to charge this very lovely woman with murder.

In poking around, Russo learned that Martin Balda, Manning's business partner who had inherited Manning's half of their import-export business, had made some poor investments and was in serious financial straits. He also learned that Balda's wife Lynda had been on the verge of leaving him, but had now – since Manning's death – changed her mind. He'd seen a picture of Lynda. She was a babe. A typical trophy, half Balda's age. He made an appointment to visit her.

"Come in," Lynda greeted Russo when he arrived at the Baldas' Portland Heights home. Everything about her was seductive. Her voice was soft. Warm. Her hair, a rippling cascade of molten pearls. The jade green velour jumpsuit that draped her small rounded body exactly matched her eyes, eyes that were in such stark contrast to the rest of her image that Russo felt startled by them. After a moment or two he realized that their color was the effect of contact lenses, but that did not alter the impression they made, that the windows into this woman's soul were closed.

Lynda ushered Russo into the living room and offered him coffee, which he accepted. "Now," she said when the preliminaries were complete. "What can I do for you?"

Lots of things, thought Russo, but he said, "Well, I understand that you and your husband were more than just business associates with the Mannings. That you were close friends as well."

"That's true," Lynda told him. "Martin and Gil were friends even before they went into business together 25 years ago."

"How about you and Margaret Manning?"

"We got along. She's a very charming woman. She gets along with everyone."

"But you wouldn't characterize your relationship as a friendship."

"Probably not."

"Nevertheless, I suppose you have some impression of the Mannings as a couple, haven't you?"

"Well, yes, I guess so, insofar as they were a couple, if you know what I mean. They seemed to have grown apart."

"What makes you say that?"

"Well," Lynda started, then hesitated, examined the coral polish on her well-kept nails, then went on. "He had planned to leave her, you know."

"No, I didn't know. Did Mrs. Manning know?"

"Yes, but she threatened to ruin him if he tried for a divorce. He was trying to work things out with her."

Russo made a note on his pad, giving himself time to think. "I understand," he said, looking straight into those jade-colored eyes, "that you had planned to leave your husband, but have changed your mind. Is that a coincidence?"

Lynda sipped her coffee and set the cup carefully, precisely back into its saucer. "No," she said at last. "Gil and I were in love."

Russo drummed absently on his notebook with the end of his pen and looked at her from under his grey, bristly brows. "I guess that's about all for now," he said.

Lynda saw him to the door, but he turned there and asked, "Do you think Margaret Manning capable of murdering her husband?"

Lynda thought a moment. "I don't know," she said. "I guess we never really know about anyone, do we, Lieutenant?"

Russo gave her an enigmatic smile, said good-bye, and left her, but sat in his car for a long while thinking of motives. Margaret might have wanted to kill Gilbert out of jealousy and rage, but one would expect her to put the poison into something that he would normally ingest. Martin had jealousy and greed as motives, but he wouldn't put barium salts into Margaret's baking soda. Lynda had reason to want Margaret out of the picture – and unless I miss my guess, she's perfectly capable, but … but so did Gilbert, and he had the opportunity. Russo thought he had the answer, but now to prove it.

When he got back to his office, Russo had a message from Margaret. He called her, then went to see her.

"I didn't want to tell you this, Lieutenant," Margaret said when they were settled in their chairs, "but Gilbert … well, Gilbert was having an affaire with his partner's wife."

"I know," said Russo. "She told me."

"Did she also tell you that I wouldn't give him a divorce?"

"Yes."

"Lieutenant, poor Gil was absolutely crazy about that woman, but I thought … well, I thought if I just hung in there, it would pass. He'd get over it. We've been through these things before, you see."

"Do you believe your husband put the barium in your baking soda thinking to poison you?"

Margaret looked at him with eyes full of tears. Her chin quivered so that she could barely speak, but she finally uttered one word, "Yes."

Russo stood. "This must be very hard for you, Mrs. Manning," he said, "but it's obvious that that's what must have happened. I believe we can call this case closed and you can begin to put your life together again."

Margaret made to rise, but Russo patted her hand. "Don't bother," he said. "I'll see myself out."

But he didn't. He opened and closed the front door, but remained inside. A mirror in the foyer gave him a view of Margaret Manning as she rose gaily from her chair, flung out her arms and spun around the room.

A moment later, she picked up the phone, pecked in a number and waited. "Hello, darling," she said, then. "Come on over. I'll open the champagne. Yes, it worked, just as you said it would. We did it. We're free and we have all the money. Well, yes, there is Lynda, but you have all the goods on her. She won't be able to claim a nickel. Yes, Martin, I love you too."

As Margaret replaced the phone, Russo stepped into the room, clasped handcuffs on her wrists, and read her her Miranda rights. "Just have a seat here, Mrs. Manning," he said. "I'll call for a squad car, we'll wait for your boyfriend, and then we can all celebrate."

TROPHIES
Based on: Tiger, Finis, Aghast, Nephew

Agatha, aghast at the news that her favorite nephew had shot a tiger, was ready to call their relationship finis.

"How could you do such a thing, Tommy?" she railed at him with hot, angry tears blurring her vision of his trophy, spread so triumphantly on his living room floor. "How could you possibly see this magnificent creature, this embodiment of graceful motion, this prime element of his habitat and want to–"

"Auntie, Auntie," soothed her nephew. "It was him or me. Honestly it was. Would you rather that I should have been his breakfast?"

"If you hadn't been there hunting him, he wouldn't have been a threat to you," she argued.

"But it's a sport, don't you see? It's–"

"Of course I see! I see all too well that you have nothing better to do with your time and my money than to travel halfway around the world to shoot innocent animals."

"Oh, it's that again, is it? Well, if that's the way you feel, if you think you should dictate every move I make, you can just take your money and…."

Agatha stiffened at this oft repeated threat, fearing that this time he might mean it.

Tom hesitated, choosing his tack carefully, then decided not to chance cutting off his cash supply with his pride. He sat down beside her and placed a comforting hand on her shoulder. "I'm sorry, Auntie," he said. "I didn't mean that. It's just that I'm a

111

grown man now and I have a right to make my own decisions."

Agatha, sensing a critical moment here, looked at him sternly. "Yes, you're right," she said. "You are a grown man. It's time you stood on your own well-shod feet and started taking the responsibilities of that exalted status."

With that, she stood, adjusted her mink stole, picked up her alligator handbag, and strode from the room.

"Aunt Agatha...." Tom pleaded, following her into the entry hall, but she gave him no heed, not even a glance, as she opened the front door, walked out, and closed it firmly behind her.

Agatha went home, then, feeling an emptiness that reached from her heart into her very soul. She'd loved that boy since he was a baby. He'd been the repository of all that she would have liked to give a child of her own, if she'd had one. She'd provided for him all of the things, all of the opportunities, his father, her brother, could not. She had suspected for a long time, however, that Tom lacked the values that would make him the kind of man she wished him to be. Somehow, his killing that tiger – for sport – epitomized not only his uselessness, but his destructiveness. She felt devastated by it.

Hanging her mink stole in her bedroom closet, she caressed its soft fur, and that of a silver fox coat next to it. She kicked off the alligator shoes that matched her bag, and removed her natural pearl necklace and earrings. She turned on her gas-log fire and pressed a button on her intercom to the kitchen. "Would you bring me a cup of tea, Alice," she said into it, then sat in her armchair beside the fire.

When her tea was brought, she thanked Alice for it, then sat alone, sipping the hot brew and gazing into the tame fire, longing for warmth. After several minutes, she went to the closet, retrieved her stole and cuddled it over herself as she resumed her seat. Still, comfort would not come. None of her luxuries could replace Tom.

As she sat there thinking of him and his tiger, thinking of her outrage, she stroked the soft mink fur. Her eyes idly found her shoes, lying discarded on the floor, her bag, tossed carelessly onto her bed. These were her trophies, her status symbols. But what did they symbolize? My wealth, she decided. The wealth I won after divorcing my successful husband. Not my courage or my skill, or even my love, for there was little of that in my marriage; I was, myself, a trophy. A trophy of my husband's success.

And what of Tom? she asked herself. Have I not tried to make a trophy of him? Have I not used my money to control him? Own him? Buy his love? And what has he done that I have not? At least his trophy was won with his courage, his energy, with the risk of his life.

Agatha lifted the fur stole from her lap and looked at it. All these poor little mink died to make this stole for me, and all I did was to write a check. No risk, no skill involved.

Her mind turned again to Tom. Tom is not dead, she reflected, as these mink are, as his tiger is. He has merely been trapped by my indulgence. I'm right to set him free, but wrong to do so in anger and hypocrisy.

Wrapping her arms around her stole and hugging it to her as though it were her beloved nephew, she made a decision. She would release him from his gilded cage, but with a final gift of love. Moving to her desk, Agatha wrote a sizeable check made out to Tom, and then a note.

"Dear Tom," it read. "It was I who unwittingly taught you to collect trophies by making you one of mine. Fortunately, I merely kept you captive. I hope this final check will ease your entry to the wilderness of real life. Please let me know how you fare; I will always care."

She looked, then, at a picture of Tom that she kept on her desk and murmured, I think you'll survive, Tom, but I'm not so sure that I will.

PERSEVERANCE WINS
Based on: Crown, Bound. Decade. Future

A bright future loomed for Annie Landry, bound to crown a decade of work with well-earned success.

It was a courageous decicion for Annie, a thirty-two-year old single mother of two boys, Greg and Bobby, aged ten and twelve, to go to college, earn a degree, and become a department store manager. Her family scoffed at her dream and refused support, but inquiries at the local community college brought her the encouragement she needed, as well as help with funding.

Even at that, she found she couldn't carry a full load at school and still work enough hours at Petrie's Emporium to support herself and her sons, so the two-year program took three years for her to complete. It seemed there were never enough hours in the day or enough dollars in the bank. It broke her heart to tell the boys she had no time for Little League games and no money for the expensive shoes and equipment they wanted. She had to restrict their clothing choices to Petrie's, where she had an employee discount, or to thrift stores. Their 7 a.m. breakfasts served as family time for them. Annie listened carefully for clues to their feelings and concerns, but found few remedies for either. It made her worry. It reinforced her guilt at sacrificing their welfare to her dreams.

Course work came fairly easily to Annie. She was bright, she loved her subject, and her years in retail work paid off here because she'd observed enough to make it relevant. She carried a 4.0 grade point average throughout.

Graduation to the university posed a giant challenge. The higher tuition, the threat of more difficult course work, the increased travel time seemed insurmountable. Moreover, the store offered a promotion in light of her newly earned certificate from the community college. It would mean more money, but it was a full-time job. It would mean giving up her dreams of earning a degree, of ever being in full charge of an entire store, of ever building that store into the shoppers' paradise she thought a department store should be. In exchange, she would have more time and more money for her boys. She could make a better home, be a better mother. She could get more sleep.

It was a soccer game that finally tipped her over. This was the first game she'd had time to attend since she'd started school. Bobby, now fifteen, made three goals. She and Greg cheered in unison and hugged each other in their excitement. Afterward, they all went to McDonald's to celebrate the victory. They were a family. She could no longer sacrifice her children and her participation in their lives to her dreams. She took the job.

But that was not the end. By September, she had a plan. She'd take one course at a time. That would mean two evenings a week away from home. It would mean a tighter budget. It would mean more stress. But it would mean progress.

Three years passed this way. Bobby graduated high school, got a part-time job, and started community college. He wanted to be an engineer. Greg was sixteen and worked after school. It was time for Annie to shift gears.

A full scholarship, complete with stipend, allowed her to go back to part-time work at the store. The next four years seemed a breeze in comparison to the previous six. She earned her B.A., then her M.B.A. She received several job offers. The best was a brand new store in a brand new mall, but two thousand miles away.

"Go for it, Mom," the boys urged her, and she did. She took the reins of that new store and built it into such a model of retailing success that ten years later, she became CEO of the entire chain.

"I only wish I could have given you the benefit of all this while you were growing up," she said to the boys as they admired her new lifestyle.

"Maybe what you did give us, the example of someone who doesn't give up, was more important," observed Bob, now a successful civil engineer who supervises projects all over the world.

Greg, now known as Dr. Landry, heart specialist, agreed.

HENRI FINDS ADVENTURE
Based on: Feign, Franc, Harrow, Safari

As a dutiful son, Henri tried to feign contentment as he towed a harrow over his father's fields for one franc a day, but his dreams were of sailing the seas in search of undiscovered lands and of trekking through dark jungles on safari.

They were not without benefit to Henri, these dreams of his, for they carried him away from the boredom of guiding his old horse in endless lines over the roughly plowed ground. His discomforts became part of the game. Wind and rain became gales at sea, and he imagined himself lashed to the helm, battling to keep his ship on course, even as he urged his horse ever forward. Heat and stinging flies became simply realities of the steamy jungle, parts of the adventure of the hunt. The prize to be won from these ordeals varied. Sometimes it was a tiger or an elephant that would become his friend. Sometimes it was an island kingdom where he would have servants to bring him sweets and cool drinks, and where everyone would have to do exactly as he said. But mostly it was simply the thought of being somewhere else that enchanted him.

Then one day, as he sat on a hummock, letting his horse rest and refreshing himself with the bread and cheese that his mother had packed for him, two men appeared as if from nowhere. They spoke to him in French, but in accents he had never heard before. They were finely dressed by his standards, wearing well-tailored white slacks and colorful silk shirts.

They smiled at him and stood with their feet wide apart, their

117

arms folded across their chests. "What is your name, young man?" asked the taller of the two.

"I am Henri DuLac," said the boy. "My father owns this land. Do you wish to see him?"

"No, not for now," said the man. "It is you that interests us for the present. When we want your father, we know where to find him."

Something in the manner of this man – the expression in his eyes, his tone of voice – aroused fear in Henri. He stood and looked around him, measuring in his mind his chances for escape.

"Don't be afraid, young Henri," said the shorter man. "We just want to take you on a little adventure. I'll bet you've been dreaming about that all your life, haven't you? Stuck out here on this farm. Leading that old horse across a field all day."

Henri looked at the man warily, wondering how he could know of his daydreams. He had never shared his secret thoughts with anyone.

"Come on," said the taller man. "Come with us. We want to take you for a ride in our fast car. We will take you to the sea. You will cruise the Mediterranian. Maybe even catch a fish. You'd like that, wouldn't you?"

Henri thought quickly. "I have to ask my parents," he said. "They might let me go if they see what fine people you are."

"No," said the short man. "You are, what, twelve years old? You can decide for yourself."

"I'm ten," said Henri.

"No matter," said the short man. "You will either decide for yourself or we will decide for you."

The tall man smiled slyly. "If you cooperate with us, you can have a very good time of this. Otherwise, you can be made quite uncomfortable."

The short man pulled a knife from his pocket, flicked open its blade, and brandished it, as the tall man suddenly grabbed

Henri's wrists and twisted him around in such a way that he was held fast, with the man standing behind him, pulling his arms crosswise of his chest.

Henri struggled and began to yell. "Papa! Papa!" he cried, but knew no one would hear him.

"Now it's like I said, son," said the short man. "You can make this very easy, or you can make it hard. Either way, you're coming with us, and you'll stay with us until your father pays us a million francs."

"But my father doesn't have a million francs," Henri protested.

"We'll see," said the short man. "Now, how's it going to be with you, young Henri?"

Henri decided that his best bet was to cooperate and watch for his chance to escape, so he pretended to relax. "I'll be able to walk better if this guy lets go of me," he said.

The short man nodded and gestured for the tall one to let the boy go, and the three of them walked to the elegant car that waited in the lane. The tall man ushered Henri into the backseat and got in beside him. The short man opened the front passenger door and said something to the driver in a strange language as he started to get in.

Suddenly, it was as though war had broken out in that quiet country lane. Black police cars raced from behind trees to block the kidnappers' car, and men in uniform swarmed in with guns drawn. One grabbed the short man while another hauled the tall man from the backseat. Henri sat bewildered, wondering what to do.

Within five minutes it was all over, and most everyone was gone. One police car remained, and one of its men walked over to the kidnappers' car to speak to Henri.

"Are you okay?" he asked.

Henri nodded, looking pale.

"Would you like us to take you home?"

Henri thought a minute, but then shook his head. "No thank

you," he said, but I would like to know…. Well, you know."

Well," said the policeman, "That short man's girlfriend tipped us off, we followed, waited, and watched. We had to let them take you, or we couldn't have arrested them."

"Oh," said Henry, and he fell silent for a minute, thinking all of that over. "Well, thank you very much," he said simply.

The policeman smiled and touched his fingers to the visor of his cap. "Are you sure you don't want us to take you home?" he asked.

"No thank you," said Henri. "I have my horse out here."

The policemen left, then, and Henri was alone. He sat there a while, feeling a little numb, but then made his way back into the field, picked up the rein of his horse, and went on with his harrowing. He'd had enough adventure to last him for quite a while.

LOVE IS INCOMPREHENSIBLE
Based on: Envoy, Vixen, Varied, Temper

That Princess Zara of Latavia was a vixen with a violent temper was a reputation that never varied, and to be sent to that country as an envoy was a dreaded assignment. Nevertheless, envoys did come from far and near to bend the ear of her father, King Dondo, begging for supplies of a secret chemical, known today as Miracle Gro, but which they called Furgli.

Now, King Dondo was a mild-mannered and reasonable man, whose tiny country had, thanks largely to Furgli, grown rich and had remained free of military conflict for centuries. Its pasturelands were green and lush, its farms and orchards bountiful. The long-haired goats native to the land produced not only abundant silky wool, from which several types of luxurious fabrics were woven, but creamy milk for the manufacture of extraordinary cheeses. Latavia's people were healthy, happy, and industrious. All except Princess Zara.

"What gets into that girl?" wondered the king as he watched his daughter flaunt her shapely body about the court and the countryside, tempting young men with her flashing dark eyes, laughing and teasing and tossing her luxurient black curls, then suddenly flying into a fury, striking and cursing the very men she'd taunted.

Wicked as his daughter appeared, however, and sincerely as he might deplore her behavior, she did serve one very important function for the king: She chased away the envoys who were constantly bedeviling him with their pleas for Furgli. "I haven't the heart to send all of these poor wretches away, but if I sold Furgli to one, I'd have to sell to all. Latavia would have none for itself, and would lose its prosperity," he reasoned publicly. Privately, he acknowledged Zara as his main line of defense. Nevertheless, because he loved Zara dearly, he longed for a cure for the unhappiness he believed to be the root of her conduct.

Meanwhile, in the far-away land of Tor, another king prepared his son, Glan, for a visit to Latavia.

"The way I see it," said that king, "is that in order to win the right to buy Furgli, we must win the hand of the Princess Zara."

"And you expect me to do that?" asked Glan.

"I do," said the king, "but it will require you to be very strong and very brave. First, you will need strength to resist Zara's charms, which we are told are very tempting. If you can do that, she will be intrigued, then frustrated, and eventually furious. That is when you will need bravery. You cannot strike back at her; you must simply take whatever she dishes out, and…." here the king paused to snicker at his own little joke, "…I hear that crockery is her favorite weapon."

The prince smiled wanly. "But then what, father?"

"Why," said the king, "when her fury is spent, you simply say, "Zara, you are magnificent. Marry me and I will supply you with the finest china to throw at me."

"So you expect me to actually marry this monster," asked Glan.

"It's your duty, son. Noblesse oblige and all that, you know," answered his father. "We need some of that Furgli stuff."

So, off went Glan, armed with patriotic zeal and his father's advice. He was received at King Dondo's palace with the courtesy due his rank, and ushered into the presence of the king and his daughter.

All of Zara' senses went atingle the moment she laid eyes on Glan, for he was indeed a handsome young man of obvious spirit and wit. For his part, Glan had a considerable struggle to keep his eyes off of Zara, whose beauty and provocative gestures made her all but irresistible. He succeeded, however, and in the days that followed, Zara's behavior became more and more sexually blatant as she tried harder and harder to capture this young man's attention.

Soon, frustration gave way to anger and on the third day, seeing Glan pass by her veranda with his attention glued strictly to the king's recitation of his country's virtues, she threw a porcelain statuette at him. Her aim was good. Her missile hit him on the shoulder. He ignored it and walked on.

"How dare he!" cried the princess, and ordered Glan summoned into her presence, whereupon she bombarded him first with venomous words, then with crockery, then with fists.

"Magnificent!" Glan declared when she collapsed in exhaustion. "Marry me and you shall have nothing but Dresden and Spode to throw at me! I shall call upon my warriers to learn battle technique from you! I shall exhibit your virtue as the finest example of womanhood!"

Zara, having crumpled in sobs at his feet, looked up at Glan with tears flooding her eyes, but a timid smile quivering at one corner of her mouth.

Glan held out a hand to help her to her feet. "But right now, you're a mess," he said. "Make yourself presentable, and I'll meet you in the throne room. In the meantime, I'll speak to your father."

Zara did as she was bidden, and in due course, Glan carried her off to Tor, together with a promise from King Dondo for all of the Fugli his country should ever need.

And did Zara and Glan live happily ever after? Yes, they did. Zara didn't change an atom of her character, though now she saved it all for Glan. Glan calmy adored her and kept all of his promises.

MORALITY AND THE PRESS
Based on: Stung, Often, Outwit, Fourth

That people who try to outwit the Fourth Estate often get stung is a lesson a would-be senator from Oregon learned painfully.

Eric Hooper was an unknown, you see, running on the ticket of the newly formed and scantly funded Morality Party. It was the belief of this party that immorality in general, and particularly sexual immorality among government officials was at the bottom of most of our country's ills. Having started out as a small-town cult with Eric as its self-styled guru, it had come to the collective conclusion that the only way to battle this blight was to infiltrate the government at its highest possible level.

Now, Eric was a charismatic fellow of 42, who had blown into Durbin – population 435 – about a year before, and immediately started talking to people about his beliefs and his dreams. He started out at the coffee shop and the barber shop. He got himself invited to speak at the Women's Club. His large solid build, thick blond hair, and piercing blue eyes gave him an aura of glamour. His warm smile and habit of looking directly into the eyes of whomever he talked with won the ladies' hearts completely. The men were a little harder sell, but many basically agreed with most of his theories, so were gradually brought into the fold until he had a following of about 60 people.

One of these was Phoebe Larkin, editor of the expanded newsletter that passed for a weekly newspaper in Durbin. Before long, a passionate missive from Eric became a regular feature.

Now, Phoebe was a happily married lady of 60 or so, so she

wasn't vulnerble to romantic notions about Eric for herself, but she had a 38-year-old daughter, Angie, who was a journalist with the *Oregonian* in Portland. What could be nicer, thought Phoebe, than to bring these two lovely people together. Angie could help Eric get the statewide coverage he deserved for his convictions and ... who could say where that might lead.

Maybe it wasn't really Eric's fault that Angie fell headlong into love, for he was careful not to make any promises to her. Nevertheless, he accepted invitations to Sunday diner at Phoebe's house whenever Angie would be there, which became more and more often. When they were alone, he didn't speak of romance to her, but, arresting her with his eyes, told her of his life and of his ideas and dreams for the moral redemption of the government and of the nation. Angie was captivated, and before long, she and Phoebe instigated Eric's little band of followers to become a political party and back him for the U. S. Senate.

It was only now that Angie and Phoebe began to check out the stories that Eric had told them. It was not at all that they disbelieved him, but they wanted more material. They wanted more people who would come forth in his support. What they found, at first, was a dead end. No one had ever heard of Eric Hooper except by reading what Angie had managed to get into the *Oregonian*. Then, gradually, a pattern began to emerge of a string of aliases, a string of swindlings of generous, believing women who had given their money and their hearts to this man, and to a group of sincere men who had supported him and been left with an empty treasury when he suddenly disappeared.

Now it was clear to Angie why Eric had been so shy of having his picture taken, and her reaction was immediate. She published his picture and a complete expose of this man and his activities. It hit the front page of the *Oregonian* and was picked up by the wire services. Eric became famous in a way he had never planned.

Eric quickly saw the handwriting on the wall, changed his

name again, and headed for South America. There, he went on as before, breaking hearts and charming people out of their hard-earned cash, but never again did he try playing games with a journalist.

THE COACH PICKS A TEAM
Based on: Coach, Fever, Realty, Notify

When word reached the suburban town of Lake Blythe that the new high school football coach would be a handsome forty-year-old bachelor named Mike Hagen, every female realty agent in town was in a fever to notify him of her qualifications to find him a home. Forewarned by a plethora of letters from these eager ladies, and determined to avoid making a circus of his arrival in his new city, Mike accepted an invitation to stay with a sedate older couple, Frank and Betty Lawson.

Frank, a retired banker and avid football fan, had been chairman of the committee that had chosen Mike as the new coach. Betty was a plump, comfortable mother-hen kind of woman who took Mike immediately into her home and her heart. The Lawson home was a commodious old house overlooking the lake and Mike was given the guest suite, which included a sitting room, bedroom, and bath.

When Mike told Betty at dinner, on their first evening together, how pleased he was with their hospitable accommodations, she responded with an affectionate smile.

"Well, it's yours for as long as you want it, Mike, so you needn't be in a hurry to find yourself any other home," she said.

"Right," Frank agreed. "Just take some time to reconnoiter. You'll have enough to do to get settled in with the team."

Mike smiled knowingly. "You're right, and I'm grateful," he said. "I just hope I won't have to wear dark glasses to hide from the realtors."

"Just tell them your not in the market yet," Frank advised. "They'll cool off after while."

"And when you're ready, Frank can put you in touch with someone sensible," Betty added.

"And a nice sensible bank, I hope," Mike said, laughing. "I think these local ladies have an inflated idea of a coach's income."

Frank gave him a wink and a nod as they all rose. "Your job is your main concern, Mike," he said. "Everything else will fall into place. For the time being, our home is yours."

Mike excused himself and went to his rooms shortly after that, and Frank and Betty retired. When the lights were out, Betty snuggled up to Frank. "Isn't he just the most delightful young man?" she asked. "Has he ever been married?"

"You were a wonder not to have asked him," said Frank with a smile in his voice.

"I know. I had to bite my tongue all evening."

There was a longish pause, and Frank's breathing became deep and even.

"Frank?" urged Betty with a nudge of her chin on his shoulder.

"Hm-m-m?" Frank murmured.

"You haven't answered me."

"Answered what?"

"Has he been married?"

"I don't know. I don't think so. It never came up."

"Well, a nice young man like that should have a wife," Betty averred.

"He's a football coach. He needs his sleep. Men with wives don't get to sleep," Frank grumbled teasingly. He gave Betty a kiss and a pat and turned over. "Good night, honey," he ended. He would like to have admonished her not to get herself involved in Mike's love life, but knew it would only lead to argument and wouldn't do any good.

Within days, Betty was telling her friends, "It's just such a delight to have Mike with us. He's so dear to me and such a joy to Frank. They talk on and on about football strategies. It's like having our own son back in the house again – only better. Mike is neat as a pin. I don't go into his rooms, of course, but the maid does, and she says his bed's always made and there's never so much as a stray sock lying around."

"How come he's single?" they invariably wanted to know, and Betty was at a loss to tell them. Nevertheless she had come to the conclusion that Mike would be a perfect match for her dear friend Kate Prentiss, the single mother of two adorable little boys.

At last, late one evening after about three weeks, Betty and Mike were alone in the kitchen. Mike had been detained at a meeting and had missed dinner, so she was making him a salad and an omelet. She sat down with him at the kitchen table as he ate. She said nothing for a time, just enjoying the presence of this large, compactly built young man with his outdoorsy complexion, his warm brown eyes, and his chestnut hair that showed just a hint of silver at the temples. She watched the manly grace of his hands and wondered again how he'd escaped the tender trap – or if he had.

"So, Mike," she said with what she hoped was an off-hand tone, "how is it that an eligible bachelor like you is still running around loose?"

Mike laughed. "I wondered when you'd get around to asking that," he said. "It's taken an admirably long time."

Betty blushed, sipped her coffee to hide it, and waited for him to go on. "Well?" she urged when he didn't.

"I'm thinking," he said, smiling, and then went on. "I guess it's mainly been that I've moved around so much, Betty. First, in the Navy, then at college, then as my career has moved me. Everywhere I go, there's some sweet lady like you who tries to fix me up, and – well, I don't think I really resist, but then along comes another move and I've escaped again."

"I haven't tried to fix you up, Mike," Betty demurred.

"Yet," added Mike, and Betty giggled.

"Seriously," Mike went on, "I do think it's about time I settled down. If I'm ever going to have a family of my own, I need to be about it, but just now I'm trying to concentrate on my job."

"I understand that, but – well, would you mind if I invited a young lady to join us for dinner now and then?"

"That's deadly!" said Mike with a laugh. "Why not wait till summer, when I've got my own digs. You can invite me to a barbecue or something."

Betty smiled surrender, but her mind was clicking on.

Mike had finished his repast by now, and took his dishes to the sink, rinsed them, and set them in the dishwasher as Betty looked on with approving eyes. He dropped an arm around her shoulders as they turned out the lights and left the kitchen. "Incidentally," he said. "Thanks for fielding those calls from realtors. It's a big help."

"Not at all," said Betty, "I'm glad to do it." She meant that sincerely. She had plans for Mike and didn't want any predatory females gumming up the works. She was glad they'd had this little talk and felt optimistic. The question, now, was how to go about it. She and Mike said good-night in the hallway and she went on to the den to knit, to wait for Frank to come home from his poker game, and to think.

Mike went upstairs to his rooms and tried to read, but something was bothering him. If he'd analyzed what he'd just said to Betty – about having "escaped again," he might have recognized a recurrent feeling of being managed or led into a trap. He could have admitted that for most of his life he'd had a sense of having women and girls grab on to him for one reason or another. He'd always felt that he was chosen; that he'd never made a choice of his own. He'd enjoyed the attention and the popularity, but the moment he felt that he was losing control or getting in too deeply, he'd run. That was the urge he was feeling now. He looked around at his comfortable surroundings and made up his mind. It was time for him to move into a place of his own.

Betty was thunderstruck when he told her the next afternoon that he'd found an apartment and would be moving the next Saturday. "You know there's no reason for you to do that, Mike. Frank and I love having you here," she told him, and he knew she meant it and felt hurt at his leaving.

"Both of you have been wonderful and I'm really grateful for your friendship and the chance you've given me to get settled in my job and familiar with the town," he said. "I just feel it's time. Please understand. My apartment is only five minutes away, you know."

There was nothing much Betty could say, but her mind raced to find a way of getting Mike and Kate together before he left.

Thus it was that on the next Wednesday afternoon Mike came home to find Betty knitting in her chair in the den and two little boys playing with toy cars on the rug. Betty greeted him and the boys stopped their play to stare at this large intruder.

Mike returned Betty's greeting and turned to the boys with a friendly grin. "Hi," he said. "I'm Mike. I live here."

"Hi, Mike," said the older of the two boys. "I'm Dave. I'm seven."

The younger boy piped up, then. "I'm Stevie," he said. "I'm five," and he held up his fingers to prove it.

"Do you want to play?" asked Dave.

"Sure," said Mike, and he got down on his hands and knees.

"You can have this car," said Stevie, handing him a green Jeep that was larger than the race cars they had. "You're bigger, so you need a bigger car."

"Right," said Mike, "and I'm gonna get in my big car and run right over you little guys."

"You have to catch us first," said Dave, racing his car quickly away with Mike in hot pursuit. "If I get to the edge of the rug, you can't touch me," Dave challenged just as he reached the

131

safety line.

"You're too quick for me," said Mike. "Maybe I can catch Stevie." As he started after him, Stevie scrambled, laughing, for the rug edge too, and got away.

They played in this way for several minutes, with the boys taunting Mike, and Mike pretending frustration at not being able to catch them. Suddenly, then, the boys jumped up and ran to a pretty blonde woman who'd just come into the room.

"Mommy! Mommy!" they cried and she knelt and gathered them into her arms.

After a couple of minutes of hugs and kisses, Stevie turned and pointed to Mike. "That's Mike," he said. "He's neat."

The woman smiled and rose. "Hi," she said. "I'm Kate Prentiss."

"Hi," said Mike. "Great little guys you have here."

"I think so," she said, and turned her attention to Betty, who had left her chair and was standing nearby. "Betty, thank you for keeping the boys for me. It was a godsend that you could take them."

"I loved having them," said Betty, "and from what I gather, so did Mike."

"Apparently," Kate said with another smile at Mike. "You must be the Mike Hagen I've been hearing about."

"Guilty," said Mike. "What have you heard?"

"Oh, just that you're the new football coach and that you've been staying with Frank and Betty."

"All true," said Mike.

Kate turned now to the boys. "Pick up your toys, guys," she said, "we have to fly."

"Oh," pleaded Betty, "can't you stay to dinner? I thought–"

"That's so sweet of you, Betty, but I really can't. I have a ton of papers to correct tonight."

"Oh dear! Well...."

"Give Aunt Betty a hug," Kate told the boys, "then head for

the car."

Two minutes more, and they were all three out the door.

"Nice little family," said Mike.

"Yes," said Betty. "Kate does a wonderful job with them. She's been alone since Stevie was a year old. We all try to be helpful when we can, but she still has quite a load."

"She said she had papers to correct. Is she a teacher?"

"Yes. Fifth grade at Blythe Elementary." Betty stood for a long minute, staring into space, trying to think what more she dared say just now, but finally said, "Well! I need to see about dinner."

"And I have work of my own to do," said Mike, and he headed for the stairs.

"Darn, darn, darn!" said Betty as she tied her apron around her middle, but she needn't have been so dismayed. Mike had been mightily impressed by Ms. Prentiss, and was at this very moment looking for her number in the phone book.

True, he did move into his new apartment on that following Saturday, so it was difficult for Betty to observe the progress of the ball she had pressed into motion, but the ball did roll forward. On the Sunday after his move, he took Kate and the boys to the zoo. On the following Wednesday, she had him in to dinner. Within a month Kate and Mike were an item. By summer, they were engaged. By fall, they were married. Betty sat by Frank's side at the wedding and held his hand fondly, happy in the secret knowledge of the part she'd played in this happy event.

As for Mike, he honestly believed that what had happened had been of his own choosing. And Kate? Well, Kate let him think so.

AFTER THE DANCE IS OVER
Based on: Chime, Glove, Daring, Lotion

As her mantel clock sounded its eight o'clock chime, Lydia Blynn finished massaging raspberry bouquet lotion into her hands and drew on a long black glove, preparing to embark on her most daring adventure in years. She was going, alone, to a singles' club dance.

As she gave herself a final once-over in the hall mirror, the dim light gleamed gently on her greying dark hair and softened the age lines around her mouth and eyes. She hoped the lighting in the dance hall would be as merciful. She practiced smiling. She'd been told she had a nice smile.

All in all, she felt pleased with her reflection. Her new short bob made her look younger than her fifty-two years; her new cobalt blue silk dress highlighted her eyes. Its softly flaring skirt flattered her roundish figure and would look pretty on the dance floor. She was as ready as she'd ever be. She picked up her keys and her black velvet evening bag from the hall table and headed for her car.

The dance was held in an old multipurpose building that housed everything from lectures and political rallies to dancing school recitals and wedding receptions. As hoped, the lighting was soft, though not dim. A trio of musicians filled the air with one of her old favorites, "Something's Gotta Give," and a few couples were dancing. Tables and chairs were arranged at either end of the room and about half were occupied by fifty or so people of about her own age, with a slight preponderance of women. Some clustered in groups, others sat apart. Most sipped drinks from clear plastic glasses and tried to look cool and confident as they stole anxious glances around the room for possible partners.

Lydia paid her twelve dollars, received her name tag and two drink tokens, then hesitated at the entrance, uncertain what to do. A tall, silver-haired man in a powder blue sport coat, whose name tag identified him as "host," greeted her with a friendly smile.

"Hello, Lydia," he said, "My name's Ralph. Can I help you get settled?"

Lydia returned his smile and nodded. "Why, yes," she said. "That would be very helpful."

Ralph escorted Lydia to the small bar set up in a corner of the room and asker her what she'd like to drink. The choice was lemonade or wine. She chose wine and surrendered a token.

"Now," said Ralph, when all of that business was taken care of, "where would you like to sit? Do you have friends here, or would you like me to introduce you to someone?"

"Oh, yes," said Lydia with gratitude. "It would be lovely to meet someone. This is my first time here, you see. I don't know a soul."

Ralph smiled. "We all know what that's like," he said. He cupped her elbow in his hand as he guided her toward a table and introduced her to Dorothy and Anne, who greeted her with fake smiles and acquiesced to Ralph's suggestion that she sit with them. Ralph pulled out a chair for Lydia, seated her, and then excused himself. "More new arrivals," he said.

Lydia watched him go. "Does he ever get to dance?" she asked.

"Eventually, once everybody gets here," said Anne, cutting a glance at Dorothy. Don't get any ideas, though. He's spoken for."

"Oh," said Lydia, blushing a bit and smiling sheepishly, "I didn't mean–"

"Oh, of course not," said Dorothy with a hint of sarcasm.

"Nobody does – much."

Anne snickered knowingly at Dorothy's remark, then turned a haughty eye toward Lydia. "Ralph is so friendly to newcomers that it's easy for them to – well, you know – I just wouldn't want you to be disappointed."

"That's very kind of you, I'm sure," said Lydia coldly, turning angrily away from the two women. "What do I have,"she grumbled under her breath, "a red 'V' for vamp emblazoned on my forehead?" Hurt by this unfriendly reception, she considered leaving the dance and going home but decided that would be silly. Instead, she simply rose from her chair, picked up her bag and her glass of wine and, without a word, began walking toward the other end of the hall.

The music had stopped and was just starting again with "Chattanooga Choo Choo" when a pudgy little man named Dale, with prominently false teeth and his hair combed sparsely across his bald dome, stopped her en route and asked her if she'd like to dance.

"Oh, dear," she stammered. "I – well I – I was just – well, not just now, thank you – I – need to – find a place to sit."

"Okay. Catch ya later, Allegator," said the little man, and he danced away with an imaginary partner.

Lydia followed him with amused eyes for a minute, shook her head, and continued on her way thinking that if nothing better happened to her this evening, just watching that kook would be worth the price of admission. Things were looking up. She found an isolated seat at the end of one of the long tables and established her place. As she sat listening to the music and watching the dancers, observing the varied personalities, she relaxed a bit and began to forget herself and the discomfort of being there alone.

The music stopped again and all at once Ralph was speaking on the microphone. "It's time for a mixer," he said. "Everybody on the floor in two circles. Ladies on the inside, gents on the outside. When the music starts, the ladies circle to the left, gents to the right. When the music stops, gents take the hands of the ladies nearest them, and lead them into the next dance."

Lydia took a sip or two of wine and went to join the inner circle. It was obvious that this game had been played many times before, for as each man passed each woman, he clasped her hand briefly before passing on to the next. It was kind of fun – almost like a folk dance – and she received several promising greetings along the way. The music stopped. Ralph held her delicate hand in his large one and flashed her a smile. "I Could Have Danced All Night" was the next selection, and as Ralph led her into it, she believed it was true. They danced as lightly and easily as though they had been partners for years.

"You changed your seat," Ralph observed after a few moments.

Lydia scrambled for a rejoinder. "You noticed," she said.

"Yes, I did. I wanted to ask you to dance."

"Oh. Well then, it's probably just as well."

Ralph looked at her askance. "What do you mean by that?"

Lydia hesitated, seeming to be lost in the rhythm of the dance, but then said, "I was told you were 'spoken for'."

Ralph rolled his eyes and laughed gently. "Well, don't believe everything you're told," he said.

Lydia sensed some kind of story behind all of this, but thought it best not to pursue it. "Okay," she said, remembering Dale's bland acceptance of facts as offered, and the two danced on.

"That was fun," Lydia said as Ralph escorted her back to her seat afterward.

"Yes it was," Ralph agreed. "Let's try it again in a bit. Now, though – sorry about this 'host' thing, but it's my job to circulate."

"I understand. It's a good thing for newcomers like myself that you do," she said as she took her seat.

"I only wish all the newcomers *were* like you," he said with a slight bow.

"Thank you, kind sir," said Lydia, and she smiled as she watched him walk away and greet someone else. What a charming man Ralph seems to be, she thought, yet she felt perplexed at what seemed to be some kind of duplicity. Dorothy must have some reason to think she had exclusive rights. Maybe lots of women – including herself, if she was not careful – were prone to mistake Ralph's professional attention as personal preference.

She sipped her wine and watched the interplay around the room and on the dance floor. Dale, she saw, was maneuvering a woman at least a foot taller than he through the intricate steps of a cha-cha-cha with style and dexterity. The woman was clearly delighted with her partner. Anne and Dorothy both danced with men who looked as though they were just in from the rodeo circuit, and who gave the dance a western flavor. Ralph was dancing with a stout woman whose whole body jiggled and bounced with the rhythm.

A man approached her with a glass in his hand. "I see your glass is empty," he said. "Can I get you something?"

Lydia was surprised by the question, but looked at her glass to find he was right. "Why, yes," she said after considering the fact that he was really asking to join her for conversation. "Wine, please," she added, offering him a token, which he accepted.

"I'll be right back," he promised, and she watched him make his way to the bar. He was a clean, blunt-looking man in chinos and a blue plaid short-sleeved sport shirt. His walk told her he probably couldn't dance worth a darn. She wondered what he was doing here. When he came back, he introduced himself as Tom and asked if he could join her. She agreed.

"I don't dance much," he said. "I hope you don't mind."

"No. I haven't danced much myself in many years."

"I saw you out there with Ralph a while ago. You were very good."

"He's very easy to dance with," she said.

"Yes."

There was a silence, then, as the two of them watched the dancers.

The music paused, and then started again with "Dancing in the Dark."

"I think I could do this one," Tom said. "Would you like to try?"

"All right," said Lydia, and he took her soft hand in his rough one as she rose, and led her to the dance floor. Within moments, Lydia knew Tom's statement about his dancing was an understatement. His flat-footed two-step seemed to have no relationship at all with the music, but they lumbered through it together to the end, when he led her back to the table.

"You were very patient," he said with a grin.

Lydia laughed gently. "Well, you warned me," she said, and he chuckled affably. "Are you a regular at these dances?" she asked.

"Pretty much, yes," he said, and when she didn't say anything, he went on. "Ralph's my older brother, and he kind of talks me into coming."

"But aren't there other activities you like better?" she asked.

"Oh sure, but most of the things I like to do are kind of solitary, like gardening and wood-working. I build custom furniture for a living. Ralph says it doesn't matter so much that I'm not a good dancer, that a lot of people come here mostly to meet other people and socialize, and I find it's true."

"I'm sure it is," said Lydia, smiling empathetically and glancing around the room.

"Lots of these ladies don't dance any better than I do," he said with a chuckle, "but we get out there and try, and then, if they're good sports, like you, we can laugh about it and have a good time."

"That we can," agreed Lydia, and then she just looked into

Tom's good-natured face. It had been a surprise to her at first, hearing that Tom was Ralph's brother, but now she could see that their resemblance lay in their easy charm.

"There's Ralph now, with Dorothy," Tom pointed out, and as Lydia looked, Dorothy glared back at her and gave her a snide grin.

"What was that all about?" asked Tom.

"I don't really know," she answered truthfully. "Ralph introduced me to Dorothy and her friend Anne when I first came in this evening, and the next thing I know, Anne is warning me to leave him alone. I didn't think that was very friendly, so I left their table. Perhaps I was rude."

Tom laughed. "Poor Ralph. He's just wants to play the field and somebody's always trying to latch onto him."

"Is that why he plays host?" asked Lydia. "So that he can flitter around like a moth?"

"A butterfly is more like it," said Tom.

"Well, if that's what makes him happy," said Lydia with a try for lightness. Nevertheless, she was reminded of her own handsome ladies' man husband who had left her a few months ago claiming the need for "space."

The music had paused again, and now she saw Ralph walking toward her. Feeling a vague panic, she glanced at her watch and said, "Oh, my! It's getting late."

Ralph arrived and put a hand on Tom's shoulder. "How's it going, little brother?" he asked.

"Oh fine. Lydia and I are having a nice time if we don't try to dance," Tom said.

"Would you let me borrow her for a few minutes?" asked Ralph.

"Sorry," said Lydia, "but I'm just ready to leave. My carriage is about to turn into a pumpkin."

Ralph glanced up at the clock over the doorway. "It's not even eleven o'clock," he said. "Surely you can stay a little longer."

She felt tempted, pleased by his coaxing, and yet afraid of the excitement his attention had produced in her. Afraid that another dance with Ralph would arouse feelings that would, in the end, cause her pain. "No. Thanks, but I really must go." She smiled at Tom. "It's been really nice chatting with you, Tom." She held out her hand to Ralph and said, "You were an excellent host."

Ralph took her hand and raised it to his lips. "Will we be seeing you again?" he asked.

Not if I have any brains, she thought, then shrugged her shoulders and smiled. "Good night," she said gently, picked up her gloves and her bag and left.

As she drove toward her home, she pondered Ralph's question. Would she go to another dance? Did she dare? Could she learn how to live like a butterfly, or would she be forever a moth, fatally attracted to men like her husband, and like Ralph? Or would she rather live with her feet on the ground, like Tom? She didn't know the answers to these questions at the moment, but now, at least, she knew she had a choice to make.

HARD WON INSPIRATION
Based on: Guise, Grimy, Beataen, Eyelid

The guise in which Tony presented himself to the innkeeper was that of a grimy derelict whose swollen eyelid and bleeding lip made him appear to have been badly beaten. In truth, he was a novelist trying to overcome a blockage in his imagination.

"What I need to do," Tony had said to his friend Gail, "is to experience a slice of life that's different enough, dramatic enough, to give me some inspiration, some new view of things. My life is just too good right now. Too placid."

"Well," suggested Gail, "I suppose you could sail out into a stormy sea in a small boat, or you could murder someone, or you could pick a fight in a redneck saloon. Any of these would give you enough action to wake you up."

Tony raised his palms toward her defensively. "Whoa," he said. "I want to wake up, not get myself killed."

"Hm-m-m," she mused. "That's going to take a little more thought.

The two of them, Gail, a slender, tan brunette in a pink bikini, and Tony, flaccid and pale in a lime-colored cotton shirt and floral-print trunks, were sitting under a teal-and-white stripped umbrella next to Tony's blue-tiled free-form swimming pool. The air smelled of coconut oil and lime. They sipped Margaritas silently for a few minutes, both letting their minds roam from their comfortable, ordered setting into the bizarre.

All at once, Gail sat up straight, set her drink on the table, and looked Tony in the eye.

"How about this," she began, and then she laid out a plan whereby Tony would be made up to look like a beaten-up street person, would seek refuge in a swank seaside inn, and let human nature take its course.

Tony listened to the plan, sipping steadily at his drink and pouring another. They discussed the where and the how, phoned a makeup artist friend, and went to work. By eleven that night, Tony was staggering into the elegant Daphne Beach Inn, wearing tattered, smelly clothing and adorned with enough fake injuries to arouse the sympathy of a stone.

The desk clerk recoiled at the sight and smell of him, but sensed that some humanitarian response was in order. Carefully keeping a discrete distance from Tony, he ushered him quickly to a small, presently vacant library adjacent to the lobby and, cringing at the thought of this creature coming into contact with the pristine off-white upholstery, invited him to sit. Leaving him, then, he bustled back to his desk and dialed 911.

Help arrived quickly. A team of paramedics hurried into the library, examined Tony's injuries, and finding them to be bogus, called the local sheriff, who ushered him none too gently into his squad car and hauled him off to the nearest pokey.

There, he was booked and shoved roughly into a cell with a couple of drunks, Leo and Gil, who, though uninjured, looked and smelled even worse than he did.

"Hey buddy," said Leo as he wobbled to Tony's side in solicitude and draped an arm around his shoulders. "What the hell's happened to you? What you doin' in jail? You need a hospital!"

Gil, meanwhile, having assessed Tony's condition in the same way, took umbrage with the policemen. "What's the matter with you guys?" he hollered. "Can't you see this guy needs doctorin'? What you treatin' him so rough for?"

"Just calm down and mind your own business, Gil," said one of the cops. "When you guys sober up and find out who this guy is, you'll be just as mad at him as we are."

Gil turned to Tony. "What's he talkin' about, Buddy? What's he blind or som'thin'?"

Tony decided it was prudent to avoid getting in any deeper with these fellow inmates, fearing that what the cop had said was true. They could indeed be pretty angry when they found out about his impersonation. Feigning pain and fatigue, therefore, he lay down on the filthy floor, closed his eyes, and began to think about his situation, the miscalculation that had gotten him into it, and what it would take to get him out of it. Leo and Gil sat down, protectively flanking either side of Tony's head and stared at him sympathetically for a while, until first Gil, then Leo slumped into noisy slumber. Tony thought of moving away from them to escape the full effects of their aroma, but, not wanting to appear unfriendly or unappreciative of their solicitude, decided to remain where he was and depend on olfactory fatigue to save him from nausea.

What he and Gail had been sure would happen when he presented himself to the reception desk at Daphne Beach Inn was that he would be summarily ejected and treated as some bit of rubbish that had washed in from the sea. There was a probability, certainly, that the police would become involved when he refused to remove himself from Daphne's doorstep, but he rather expected that the police would take his side in the matter and chide Daphne Beach Inn for its heartlessness. Maybe they'd see it as kind of funny, this successful writer pulling off a stunt like this in the interest of artistic creativity. Maybe they'd just shake their heads in bemusement and let it go at that. The worst outcome he'd seen was maybe a reprimand and a fine for causing them to be involved in a hoax. It had never occurred to either he or Gail that if the paramedics were called in, he could be responsible for their not being available for some actual emergency. He had no way of knowing if that was the case or not, but the fact that it could have been plunged him into a fit of remorse and self flagellation.

The floor was hard. Tony turned on his side and pillowed his head with his arm. He tried to ignore the stench that surrounded him even as he acknowledged his own contribution to it. He tried to let the snores of his companions lull him into sleep, but just about the time he succeeded, one of them would shift rhythm or inject a new sound and he'd be awake again.

The hours crawled by, and at last a cop came to the cell door and opened it.

"Come on, you guys," he said, shaking Gil by the shoulder. "Rise and shine. "You too, Leo. This is no rest home, you know."

The two men woke, and sat up, stretching and rubbing their eyes. Tony started to get to his feet, but the cop motioned him back down. "Not you, pal," he said. We'll deal with you later."

Leo looked up at the cop. "How about some coffee?" he said with a teasing grin.

"Sure," said the cop. "It'll be along any minute now with your bacon and eggs. Come on, you guys. On your feet. You've had all the hospitality you're going to get."

Groaning, the two got up and shuffled toward the door, where Leo turned and gave Tony a long puzzled look, shook his head, and followed his friend out of the cell. "There's som'thin' mighty funny about that guy," he mumbled.

Gil glanced back and squinted in Tony's direction. "Yeah, there is. Som'thin' just not right. Oh, well, so long, buddy. Good luck to ya," he said.

Tony raised his hand in farewell and watched as the cop clanged the cell door closed again and ushered his charges out of the cell block.

Boy, Leo sure had the right idea about that coffee, Tony thought as he took a pee in the toilet. And a shower and shave and some clean clothes wouldn't hurt either. He ran his hand over his face, feeling the remnants of the fake wounds crumble. There was no mirror over the sink, but he could imagine how he must look. He turned on the faucet and bent over the sink, splashing water copiously over his face and watching it fall black and red and yellow into the basin. When it began to run clear, he looked around for paper towels, but there were none, so he dried his face as best he could on the sleeve of his shirt. He looked at his watch. 7:14, it read, and he wondered how long it would be before they'd let him go. He wanted to call his lawyer. He wanted to call Gail. He wanted some coffee. He wanted out of here.

At last a cop, a different one, this time, entered the cell block and opened his cell door. "Come on," he said, sounding bored, and Tony followed him out to the office, where a police sergeant sat behind a high desk.

"Do you have an explanation for the stupid stunt you pulled last night?" asked the sergeant.

"Well, yes, I do, Sergeant," said Tony respectfully. "You see, I'm a novelist, and I was making a kind of sociological experiment that didn't go the way I expected it to, and, well, I'm sorry for involving you all and the paramedics and everyone. I just don't know what else to say."

"I'd suggest you think of something before you come up before the circuit judge in … let me see, here … three weeks. On the 17th. Meanwhile, you'll have to post bail of one thousand dollars."

"I don't have a check with me," said Tony.

"Well then, you'll have to stay with us until someone can bring you one," said the sergeant.

"Sure," said Tony. "My girlfriend…." Oh, God, he thought, I have no idea where Gail might be. She had dropped him off about a quarter mile from the Daphne Beach Inn and was going to meet him back there an hour or so later. Why hadn't they made a contingency plan? Well, this whole idea was dumb from the beginning. But what was he going to do now?

"Yes?" said the sergeant, with eyebrows raised expectantly.

"Yes, I'm sure my girlfriend will come looking for me sooner or later, and–"

"Well, until somebody comes up with a thousand dollars, you're just going to have to be our guest."

Tony looked helplessly at the outside door and felt beads of sweat run down his neck. "Well, sure," he said, "I guess that's logical, but … do I have to stay in the drunk tank?"

The sergeant laughed a little and said, "No, we'll put you in a holding cell. We'll even serve you a cup of coffee. On the house."

Tony smiled weakly and glanced again at the doorway just as Gail came through it. "Gail!" he cried and he grabbed her in a bear hug.

"Ugh!" she said, pushing him away from her. "You stink!"

"I know, but I'm so glad to see you. Have you got your checkbook?"

"No, but I've got my debit card. What's up? You need bail?"

"Yes. A thousand bucks."

She gave him a look and then fished in her handbag for her wallet.

"Don't look at me that way," said Tony. "This was all your idea, you know."

She met his eyes. "I know," she said sheepishly, then pulled her debit card from her wallet and offered it to the sergeant.

The several minutes it took to process the bail and do the other paperwork seemed like an hour to Tony and Gail as they stood there looking blindly around themselves, not daring to talk lest they find themselves in even more trouble. At last the sergeant handed Tony a court summons, Gail a receipt, and told them they were free to go.

Tony opened the driver's door of Gail's car for her, and made a move to kiss her as she slid behind the wheel.

"Please!" she said, avoiding his advance.

"Sorry," he said, smiling at her.

"Get in," she said. "You look like you could use some

breakfast. We can go to McDonalds' drive-up window, and then head home to your shower."

Tony barely spoke to Gail as they ate, or as she drove him home. He didn't ask her in, and he didn't answer his phone for the next ten days. Gail didn't fuss; she knew he wasn't angry, he was working. When he was finished, they'd go and celebrate with a weekend at Daphne Beach Inn, a place more hospitable to the downtrodden than they had ever imagined.

CULTURE SHOCK
Based on: Frolic, Versus, Pitted, Utterly

Congroversy among the finery-flaunting intermission crowd at Carnegie Hall pitted those who revere Igor Stravinsky so seriously that tonight's frolic through his "Firebird Symphony" seemed an insulting parody, versus those who were utterly delighted by it. Among this crowd, and caught on opposite sides of the controversy, were Carol and Doug Holland from the small but ambitious town of Riverbend, Oregon.

Carol and Doug, having grown up in Riverbend, are fairly typical of its longtime residents. Doug works in the town's lumber yard, owned by his father; Carol copes with their three children, runs the house, looks after the garden, and is active in several of the town's women's organizations. Her greatest enthusiasm of the past year or so has been the Riverbend Cultural Society, which seeks to raise the town's awareness of, and support for, such events as art shows, plays, poetry readings, and concerts. It's been a struggle because the town's natives are difficult to excite in these areas, and the more affluent, better educated newcomers are prone to turn up their noses at the Society's frankly amateurish efforts. To improve the situation, it was decided that a fund raiser would be the first order of business. A raffle – with an expense-paid luxury trip to New York City as its first prize – was set afoot. Carol, partly to set an example for others, but largely prompted by the possibility for boosting her own self-image by making such a trip, bought twenty-five tickets at five dollars apiece out of money she had set aside for a new sewing machine. Doug was not consulted.

As we can observe from the fact that Carol and Doug were among the crowd at Carnegie, Carol won. They were to fly to New York out of Portland, stay at the New York Hilton, dine at Four Seasons, visit the Metropolitan Museum of Art, attend a concert of the New York Philharmonic at Carnegie, and have some cash at hand for incidental meals during their three-day, two-night stay. Doug's reaction was, "Do we have to go?"

The days and weeks leading up to the October 25th departure threatened stress between these two hitherto compatible people. Carol could think of, and talk of, nothing else, and Doug, an easy-going sort who loved his wife, and loved peace even more, went along with it all with bland good humor. Her clothes were all wrong for New York, she declared – and so were Doug's. A shopping trip into Portland was mandatory. The *New York Times* became a staple at the breakfast table, with "must read" articles marked for Doug – which he managed to ignore most of the time.

When at last the departure date arrived, all went surprisingly well. They made their air connections easily; their luggage arrived intact; they caught the limousine to the Hilton; their room was available and agreeably posh. Then, all at once, Doug noticed a decided change in his wife. Her voice took on a haughty edge, and she spoke imperiously to the bell boy – and then to him, when, tired from the trip, he took off his jacket and shoes and stretched out on the bed.

"Doug, for heaven's sake, where do you think you are?" she demanded of him.

"Honey," he sighed patiently, "I know where we are. We're at the Hilton, and our room's paid for, and I'm tired."

Carol wrinkled her brow at him, and took another tack. "I am, too, Doug, but we didn't come all this way to lolly-gag around in our room."

"It'll be time for a drink and some dinner in an hour, and then we have to go to that concert," Doug observed, glancing at his watch. "Don't you think we ought to get some rest?"

"I think we ought to freshen up, and go out where we can see and be seen," she said with exasperation. "We aren't going to be here for a month, you know."

"Okay," he agreed reluctantly, "but I need a shower, and I should think you'd want one too. Why don't you go first while I just close my eyes for a few minutes."

Carol rolled her eyes, then looked dejectedly at the clock and realized Doug was right. There really wasn't all that much time.

An hour and a half later, they were having dinner in the hotel dining room. Carol wore her new cocktail dress and felt very full of herself, casting disparaging glances at the clothing of other diners, and whispering comments to Doug, who concentrated on his steak.

Soon, they were in a cab headed for the Carnegie. Their seats were in the third row of the first balcony, but a little too far off center to suit Carol. The concert began with Mozart and Gounod, then went on to Stravinsky. Doug relaxed and enjoyed it all, but was particularly captivated by the spirited rendition of "The Firebird." Then came intermission, and the excited controversy among audience members gathered in the foyer.

"That was terrific!" Doug enthused.

"It was awful!" objected Carol. "Poor Stravinsky! What would he think if he could hear! They've made a mockery of it with all those sound effects and antics."

Doug shrugged and looked around at the crowd, then back at her. "But it was fun, Carol. It woke everybody up. Look around! Everybody's excited. Whether they liked it or not, they're talking about it."

Carol paused and looked around them with furrowed brow. "Well, you're right about that, anyway," she said. "But is it right to – to make fun of a piece of music for the sake of – of conversation?"

Now it was Doug's turn to pause and look at the woman he'd

been married to for twelve years. "I didn't know you were so uptight," he said. "Matter of fact, since when did you become such an expert on classical music?"

Carol turned her back on him and began walking back toward their seats in the auditorium. Doug followed her sullenly and they sat, then, silently side by side, waiting for the program to resume. When it was over, they smiled stiltedly at each other and made their way out of the auditorium and eventually into a cab and back to the Hilton. Without speaking, they undressed, took their accustomed turns in the bathroom, and got into bed, back to back.

In a few minutes, Doug became aware that Carol was crying, and wondered what to do. He turned over and laid a hand on her shoulder. "Is it because I liked the 'Firebird'?" he asked.

No answer.

"Come on, honey," he said. "Talk to me. Yell at me if you want, but don't cry. This is your trip to New York. You don't want to spend it like this."

"Oh, Doug," she said. "I've just been lying here thinking about...."

"About what?" Doug prompted when she didn't go on.

"Oh, just about the way I've been acting. I've been terrible, and I haven't had any fun at all, and you – you've just been rocking along as if you're the one who's having a good time."

Doug thought a minute, then said, "Well, maybe it's just that I haven't been as excited about all this as you have. I'm not so uptight. I don't feel like I have to pretend to know anything I don't."

When Carol didn't say anything for a minute, Doug thought maybe he'd put his foot in it again, but then she turned over and put her arms around him. "You're right. That's what I've been doing. I've been trying to act like a big-city know-it-all."

Doug cuddled her closer and said, "Well, I'm sure glad you're not because if you were, you wouldn't like being the wife of a small-town lumber jockey."

Carol sat up, then, dried her eyes and blew her nose, and settled back into Doug's arms. From then on, the Hollands' trip to New York was a lot more fun.

FROM HERE TO REALITY
Based on: Incognito, Nuance, Kimono, Decipher

As an incognito deputy to Robert Andrus, the gallery owner, Sandy's job was to mingle with the guests and decipher every nuance of debate among them, but the kimono she wore caused such an uproar that most of the conversation centered upon her.

It was truly an outstanding kimono; a virtual garden embroidered on crimson silk; an obi of gold that shimmered with green. Yet it was not the costume alone that attracted such avid attention. Sandy, herself, seemed incandescent in her willowy grace. Honey-blonde hair crowned an ivory complexion that resonated with the colors of her gown. Brown eyes radiated the warmth of umber.

No one knew who she was, and few dared ask, so a single question permeated the room. Sandy was Eliza at the ball; the center of attention, obscuring the works of the three featured artists in the gallery.

Now, even these artist did not know of Sandy's official function at the exhibit, and thought her to be simply a guest. Nevertheless, when she stayed, basking in the attention given her, they began to complain to Robert that something should be done.

"No one is paying a shred of attention to my marbles," whined one of them, and the sentiment was echoed by the others. "Get rid of her!" they all agreed.

Robert gazed frantically around the room, fully aware of the problem, and fully in sympathy with the artists. He felt at a loss as to what to do, however, for he felt torn between his support for the artists and satisfaction in his own sucess in creating the sensational figure that Sandy represented.

Sandy was, to begin with, you see, Robert's cousin, the daughter of his mother's sister Grace, who was a substantial supporter of his gallery. Robert had agreed to accept Sandy as a member of his household because Grace was deeply concerned about the romance that had blossomed between Sandy and some "ne'er-do-well," and believed that by putting some thousand miles or so between them, she could squelsh it. The arrangement was fairly agreeable to Robert, who saw himself as some kind of Henry Higgins, who would groom Sandy for life, first in the artistic world, and then as the wife of some nice man of substance. The fact that Robert's volatile wife, Lillian, was more than a little displeased with the arrangement made Robert a bit more eager for accomplishment than he might otherwise have been, made him a bit overzealous. The result was Sandy, as she appeared at the gallery opening of which we speak.

Robert appraised Sandy now, as she wandered about the room, champagne glass in hand. She was indeed a lovely work of art, yet his critical eye mitigated the unbridled pride he might have felt in her. Lovely as she was, she was not having the desired effect on her admirers. Everyone was talking about her, but not to her. She seemed to be inspiring awe, but not a desire to communicate – or to woo.

Suddenly, as he watched, a new glow came to Sandy's face, and animation to her body. Her umber eyes held new fire. He followed her gaze to a newcomer to the room, a young man who appeared to have just stepped out of Greek mythology. This was Dionysus reincarnated, and he knew, now, why Aunt Grace had brought Sandy into his protection. He saw, also, observing the change in Sandy, that while moments ago she had been a magnificent mannequin, she was now an alluring woman.

Robert was not alone in these observations. A hush fell upon the room. All eyes became fastened to these two glorious young people, drawn by the magnetism between them. Panic gripped him. Not only would the artists represented at this showing be furious enough to boycott his gallery in the future and induce their friends to do likewise, but Aunt Grace would withdraw her support. None of that would be fair, of course. Robert had thought he was serving each of their best interests, as well as Sandy's, not to mention Lillian's, by playing Pygmalion with her and involving her in the gallery. It was not his fault that his plan had backfired.

Before he could think what to do, however, Sandy had taken the matter into her own lovely hands.

"Greg!" she cried in delight. "I'm so glad you've come! Look at these pastels! These marbles! These bronzes!" And taking him by the hand, she led him from space to space in the gallery, expounding as Robert had a day or so before, coached her to do. For his part, Greg fell in with the game, inventing his own comments.

The mesmerized crowd followed them and gradually allowed themselves to become inspired to transfer some of their awe to artifacts other than Sandy and Greg. Within minutes, they were chatting with the artists and with Robert. Soon, even a few purchases transpired. Sandy and Greg came to be seen as more or less mortal as they circulated, refilling champagne glasses and offering hors d'oeuvre trays.

When it was all over, Sandy, Greg, and Robert secured the gallery and retired to a nearby coffee house to talk. They settled themselves around a high, round table and exchanged impressions of the showing for a while, but then came a silence.

"So," Robert said then, "what about you two?"

Sandy and Greg looked at each other and back at Robert. "We love each other," Sandy said.

"That's not exactly a secret," Robert observed.

Sandy blushed and cut her eyes adoringly at Greg, who said, "I suppose not. It's been that way for us since we met three years ago, but Sandy's mom...."

"She seems to think you have no future, and that your relationship is purely physical," Robert said, looking Greg in the eye.

"That's because I ride a motorcycle and follow the sun," Greg said. "I'm a novelist. Mostly unpublished, I admit, but, well, I work here and there, at this and that. It's all good experience and I get by. Sandy's like me, in a way. She hasn't found her niche, but she – well, you saw her tonight. She's magnificent, and we're true partners. We inspire each other."

Robert nodded, smiling proudly at Sandy, his own creation of the evening, but then waxed serious and said, "But her mother wants her to go back to school and become her own person."

"I am my own person!" Sandy exclaimed. "And I'm certainly not going to become any more my own person by being dressed like a geisha and paraded like an hors d'oeuvre among your art mavens."

Robert felt as though his face had been slapped. "Hey!" he said, I'm just trying to do my best for everyone here."

Sandy laid a sympathetic hand on his. "I don't blame you, Robert. It was fun learning about your artists. I felt like a queen tonight. But it was all a sham. You know that. I couldn't communicate with anyone till Greg came."

"Sandy and I are a team," Greg added. "Her mom wants to split us up because she sees Sandy as – well, I guess as you did when you dressed her up like a Japanese doll." He paused here, sensing Robert's pain, then added, "Well, sorry, Sandy really was beautiful tonight, and maybe you saw something in her that had never been there before, but–"

"But I wasn't a person!" Sandy interjected. "Not until Greg walked in and I forgot about my costume. If you and Mom have your way, I'll never be me. I'll spend my life as – as Greg said – as a doll. A trophy wife."

Robert sipped his coffee and stared into his cup for a minute or two. Aunt Grace's support of his gallery was important to him, yet he saw the necessity to set this lovely twenty-three-year-old girl free to find her own way. After a moment, he slipped from his stool, placed a twenty-dollar bill on the table and said, "I give up, kids. It's up to you. If you can get along without your mother's money, so can I."

When he'd left, Sandy and Greg looked at each other with large eyes, filled with apprehension, but then smiled – tentatively, but with confidence born of love.

THE PRICE OF
ALMOND MACAROONS
Based on: Candid, Almond, Lascivious, Entire

When a lascivious-looking young man in an unbuttoned shirt walked into her bakery and wanted to buy her entire stock of ten dozen almond macaroons and pay her next week, Rosie laughed and asked if she was on *Candid Camera.*

"No!" the man assured her. "It's just that I'm in a terrible bind."

"I see," said Rosie, still suspicious of such an odd request. "So why don't you tell me about it, Mr...."

"Radcovich," supplied the man. "Randy Radcovich. You see, I'm trying to impress my girlfriend's mother, who loves almond macaroons."

"But ten dozen?" queried Rosie.

"Well, you see, I sort of told her I would make her that many for a tea she's having this afternoon."

"But you didn't make them?"

"I couldn't. I don't even own an oven."

"Well, that was pretty stupid, wasn't it?" asked Rosie with a smirk. "I still think you're from *Candid Camera.*"

"No, honestly," Randy said earnestly, "and I'm not as stupid as I look – or not quite. It's just – well – my girlfriend and I were visiting her mother the other day, talking about this and that, and she mentioned what an addict she was of almond macaroons, and, just kind of joking, said the cost of them was – in her words, 'going to be her financial ruin'. So, I said that if she would let me

159

marry Dodie, I would make her all the almond macaroons she would ever want. I figured that, after Dodie and I were married, I could probably get her to do it. After all, how hard could it be? Right?"

Rosie gave him a wry smile and cocked her head to one side as if to ask if he thought he was winning her over with that kind of flattery, but said nothing. Randy caught the message, but stumbled on with his explanation.

"Anyway, Dodie's mom was so happy with that idea that she said that if I would supply her with ten dozen macaroons for a tea she was planning, she'd not only let me marry Dodie, but she'd give us a nice nest-egg for a wedding present. All of this was just in fun, of course – or at least I thought it was. But then Dodie let me know that her mom has a kind of fetish about honesty, and that if I didn't produce, I mean actually produce ten dozen macaroons with my own vaunted culinary expertise, our romance was doomed."

"So the party's today and you've failed to come up with any macaroons and you think I should just hand you my entire stock," Rosie surmised.

"No. Well, yes, for now, but Dodie and I plan to get married this weekend, and then I'll be able to pay you. I'll pay you anything you ask," pleaded Randy.

"It didn't occur to you, I suppose, to come in here and order what you needed and make the necessary financial arrangements like any reasonable adult would do," Rosie asked.

"I just didn't know how hard it would be to find them. Do you know you're the only bakery in town who makes them?"

"Yes, I do, and I know my most consistent customer, Amy Caldwell, has a daughter named Dodie."

"Yes! That's her. That's who I'm talking about!"

Rosie pursed her lips, crossed her arms across her breast, and really looked at Randy seriously for the first time since he'd come into her shop. He was a pretty good-looking kid. Kind of sexy, with his sun-bleached hair and toothy grin. She pegged him as the kind of guy who used his looks and personality to get what he wanted, and now was going for the gold. Amy Caldwell's gold, not to mention her precious daughter.

Rosie narrowed her eyes and said, "So you think you're going go parlay ten dozen macaroons – that you manage to con out of me – for a rich woman's daughter and a cushy life from then on?"

Randy had the decency to blush, but said, "I'm not conning you, Rosie – that's your name, isn't it? This is your very own bakery?"

Rosie nodded, thinking, Yes, and it didn't get to be that way by letting guys like you charm me out of all my cookies. "Yes," she said, "I'm Rosie of Rosie's Bakery, and right now I feel like I have a chance to save a life."

"Yeah!" Randy exclaimed, smiling excitedly. "The life you'll save will be mine! I'll pay you for sure. I'll pay you double. Whatever you say!"

"Right," agreed Rosie, and she started piling macaroons into cake boxes.

"No! Wait!" Randy cried. "Not in those boxes. They have your name on them. Don't you have any plain paper bags?"

"Oh! Of course!" agreed Rosie, and transferred the macaroons into white paper sacks. Then, as Randy began gathering them into his arms, she asked, "And what will you tell Dodie's mother when she asks about the special ingredient that makes these macaroons so special?" she asked.

"Uh, I don't know," Randy admitted. "What is it?"

Rosie smiled slyly. "Well, maybe she won't ask," she said, knowing full well that Amy Caldwell would recognize Rosie's macaroons in an instant, would know Randy for the liar and cheat that he was, and would bar him from her daughter's life for evermore.

His arms full, Randy asked Rosie to open the shop door for

him. "Don't worry, Rosie," Randy said in parting, "I'll pay for these – three times over."

Rosie smiled sweetly and said, "I'm sure you will, Randy," and closed the door behind him.

THE MAGIC IS IN THE MERGER
Based on: Velvet, Prayer, Lyrics, Besotted

To have even a prayer for a chance to croon his love lyrics to the beautiful Princess Myra, the poor, romantically besotted Ambrose believed he must clothe himself in mauve velvet, Myra's favorite color and fabric, a feat that seemed beyond his dreams.

From early boyhood, Ambrose had placed himself in the first row of spectators when the royal family made a procession through his small village. Every year, he waited eagerly to see Myra's carriage roll by. Every year, he was prepared with a new song of homage to her. Every year, he waited for a pause in the procession, or at least a pause in the processional music – so that he could sing his song to her. He knew that, as a poor peasant boy, he could not hope for more than a smile, a wave, a moment of her attention, but alas, in seven years, he had not achieved even that.

At last, in the year of her sixteenth birthday, a contest was held to find the finest singers, dancers, and lute players in all the kingdom to entertain at Myra's birthday party.

Ambrose knew, from the bottom of his soul, that his music could qualify to be chosen, for it was composed of the purest love. Still, he rose early each morning and went to his secret place in the forest, where the soft sibilance of a rushing stream complemented the vibrato of his lyre and the mellow tones of his voice. The words were an outpouring of years of admiration and devotion, meant solely for the ears and the heart of his beloved Myra. Sometimes, in sheer frustration, he would cry out to the stream, the trees, and the birds and animals that surrounded him, lamenting his shabby clothing. "I can't even present myself for the competition in the clothes I have," he sobbed.

One morning, however, he was startled from his tirade by the appearance of a small, homely man, grandly dressed from head to toe in mauve velvet; precisely as he had a thousand times envisioned himself.

"Ah!" croaked the little man in a raspy voice and impatient tone. "It's you again, is it?"

Ambrose, speechlessly agape, stared at the man until the man went on.

"How many times have you come here to this glade, playing your lyre in harmony with our brook, singing such love songs that you have our young females quite in a dither?"

"I-I don't know," Ambrose stammered. "It has always been my secret place. I did not know I was disturbing anyone."

"Well, know it our not, we're tired of hearing you lamenting over such a simple problem of what you shall wear," rasped the man.

"That may be a simple problem to you," said Ambrose. "You, standing there in your beautiful mauve velvet. Are all of your people so grandly dressed?"

"Oh yes," said the man. "It is our gift, you see, just as your music, your mellow voice, and your handsome face and form are your gifts."

Ambrose sat himself on a mossy fallen tree and pondered that for a moment, but could not see where this revelation could help him.

"Maybe it would be better," he mused, "if each of us had a little of everything. That way we could all be happier."

"But if that were so," argued the man, you would have only an ordinary voice, face, and figure. You would sing ordinary songs, and the strings of your lyre would lose their magic. In fact, so would everyone become ordinary and would do only ordinary things. Would that be a good thing?"

After considering for a moment, Ambrose decided not. "No, perhaps not," he conceded, "but then, what is the answer?"

The little man climbed up onto the fallen tree alongside Ambrose and put his hand on Ambrose's shoulder. "For each of us to use the gifts we have to fill in the deficits in others, while they fill deficits for us," he said. "I think it's called 'networking' or something like that."

Ambrose's face brightened with this new idea, yet faded again in puzzlement. "How would that work?" he asked.

"Well, in our case – yours and mine, that is – you want to sing for the princess, but lack clothing. I want to provide clothing for the princess, but lack the voice and the charming words. If I dress you for the contest, and you win the attention of the princess.... Well, I'm sure you can see where this is going."

Ambrose was so delighted with this idea that a deal was struck on the spot. The little man became Ambrose's tailor; Ambrose became the little man's ambassador; Princess Myra was so delighted with the whole result that she fell in love with Ambrose, they were married, and spent the rest of their lives promoting the idea of everyone striving for excellence in gifts to be offered in support of the efforts of others. As a result, the whole kingdom became prosperous, with each person in the land achieving his or her dreams.

A GOPHER IN THE PARK
Based on: Elegant, Gopher, Bonnet, Leash

Emily, dressed carefully in an elegant frock the color of robin's egg, and a matching bonnet trimmed in eyelet embroidery, strolled through the park, leading her pet gopher, Oscar, on a leash.

The girl, herself, was enough to turn heads. The blue of her dress matched her thickly lashed eyes, and the bonnet allowed just a flirtatious glimpse of the dark curls that framed the rose-cream complexion of her face. Her gait, while leisurely and graceful, showed evidence of a lilting vitality of spirit, and her expression, as she bent her gaze on the black rodent who scurried haltingly before her, was one of amused affection.

As was to be expected, her pet drew the attention of dogs being walked in this park. They barked at him and would have attacked fiercely but for their owners, who kept them in check. Tom, however, the owner of a sassy grey Schnauzer, took a different attitude. True, he prevented his yapping dog from attacking Oscar physically, but he, himself, attacked the girl with words as sharp as his dog's.

What did she mean, he wanted to know, bringing a rodent to the park, tempting more conventional pets to unseemly behavior? Didn't she realize that the poor little beast was frightened to death? What was she, some kind of lunatic?

The girl did not answer him, but sauntered on, leaving the young man looking foolish, shouting at her calmly retreating figure until, at last realizing the futility of his attack, he fell silent.

Managing to quiet his dog, then, he set it back onto the path and continued his walk, but his mood was spoiled and he yanked impatiently at the leash whenever the Schnauzer paused.

For all the rest of the day, and all of the following week, Tom suffered the conflicting emotions of anger at Emily for bringing such a foolish pet to the park, and embarrassment and shame for what he knew in his heart was inappropriate behavior on his part.

Why had he reacted so violently when it was not at all his nature, he wondered. And why was a beautiful girl walking a gopher in the park? In the end, the second question fascinated him more than the first, so on the following Sunday he took not his Schnauzer to the park, but a single pink rose.

Meanwhile, Emily's composure had not been as complete as it had appeared. True, she had maintained her dignity under the young man's onslaught, but his words had cut her deeply. She, too, spent an agonizing week caught between anger at his effrontery and shame at the realization that he had been right, and that her motivation in bringing Oscar to the park was not affection for him, but to attract attention to herself.

Thus, on that following Sunday morning, while Tom, rose in hand, waited for her in the park, Emily pondered her possibilities: to take Oscar to the park again would be stupid; to stay away from the park altogether would be silly; to go to the park without Oscar would be to risk having that ruffian laugh at her.

So Tom, arriving at the park at about the time of their first encounter, posted himself alongside the path and waited. As the sun rose in the sky and the shadows on the lawn shortened, he began to despair of seeing her. Perhaps, he worried, she had taken his bitter words seriously after all. Perhaps he had caused her such pain that he would never see her again. The expression on his handsome face fell from high expectation to a kind of low doldrum.

At last he turned, thinking to leave, but then glanced back again just as Emily appeared, all in pink, a complement to his rose. She held no leash, led no gopher. Perhaps she had listened.

As she approached, Tom stepped into her path, smiling gently. Removing his boater and placing it over his heart, he made a slight bow as she neared him and proffered his rose to her. "In apology," he said.

"Thank you," said Emily, accepting the rose with trembling dignity, "but you see, I've decided you were right. I've learned something.

"So have I," said Tom, offering his arm. Emily laid her hand upon it and the two fell into stride for a long, long walk.

IMPOTENT PARENTHOOD
Based on: Gnarl, Wield, Purple, Resist

One system of magic that children wield over their parents is to gnarl their foreheads until their faces are all purple, and if that doesn't work, squall. A second system is to look and act so adorably that their parents can't resist them.

In illustration, is the story of two boys, Roger and Peter, born to George and Abigale Carter, two years apart. The elder, Roger, had used the first method of magic; Peter the second.

Roger had been planned into his parents' lives and they had looked forward avidly to his arrival. His system of control, however, had completely exhausted them by the time he was three months old. Moreover, assuming that his disposition was somehow their fault, they declared themselves inept parents and decided one child was all the guilt they could bear.

God, however, had other plans for them. Peter arrived, and from his earliest days delighted his parents' hearts with smiles, happy gurglings, and sleeping through the night after the first month.

As their sons grew, George and Abigale strove valiantly to love them equally. Practically speaking, of course, this translated to giving them equal amounts of their thought, time, and financial favors. But while the thought they gave Roger was concern, the thought they gave Peter was joyous appreciation. The time and gifts they gave Roger stemmed from duty and guilt; the time and money spent on Peter came from fondest love.

Because, as the boys grew from childhood into young

manhood, the patterns of their behavior remained the same, so did the patterns of their various relationships. Peter found his life exciting and everything seemed to come easily to him, from learning to read to throwing a ball. His teachers liked him, he made friends readily, and when it was time for him to find employment, he had no trouble at all, advancing quickly in his chosen profession. Roger, on the other hand, hated school, fought with his peers, never found a job he liked, and was scuttled in business by disloyal employees.

   George and Abigale watched their boys progress through their lives with a sense of bewilderment. How could they have succeeded so well with Peter and failed so miserably with Roger? They spent their golden years feeling buoyant with pride in the one; riddled with guilt with regard to the other, never questioning the extent of their responsibility for either.

MADAM VIVIAN
Based on: Viable, Prostitution, Gathered, Enterprise

"Prostitution can be a perfectly viable business enterprise," said Vivian, a smartly dressed redhead, to the half-dozen suggestively clad young women gathered around her, "and with me as your Madam, I promise you, it will be."

This was tall talk coming from someone who'd never been a prostitute and never intended to become one. She'd done a lot of thinking, though, and believed she had a plan. For her, it was not a matter of earning a livelihood for herself, but a two-pronged mission: philanthropy toward the young women she hoped to elevate, and revenge against a philandering husband. She would guide girls such as these, first to make prostitution pay, and then get out of it if they chose. In the process, she'd turn her ex-husband's pride and joy, the stately home she'd won in the divorce settlement, into a whore house.

The first thing Vivian did was to move the six girls into her spacious home and assign them bedrooms and household tasks. The girls demurred at this, but Vivian told them, "This has to be a hush-hush operation. We can't have a bunch of servants out blabbing to the neighbors. With seven of us pulling our weight, it won't be all that bad."

"But if it's hush-hush, how will we get any customers?" one girl objected.

"Did you think we were going to hang a red light out in front?" Vivian asked with a teasing smile. "You just leave that problem to me."

The next thing Vivian did was to take the girls, one by one, to re-sale clothing shops and guide their purchases toward smart, respectable-looking wardrobes. "Your allure will be in your voices and in what you say and do," Vivian told them, "not in sleazy, obvious clothing. A man will spend a lot more money to bed a lady than he will a slut."

But all of this took time. A few days of settling in and shopping and organizing the household slid into a week, then two and three. Finally, a month had elapsed and no "John" had crossed the threshold. The girls began to complain. Sure, they were living safely and eating well enough, at Vivian's expense, but they were getting bored and they weren't making any money.

"You're not ready yet," Vivian kept telling them, but actually, she was stymied. She hadn't the least idea of how to start the business end of this enterprise.

But then an idea struck: "While you're completing your training – and to help it along–" she said to the girls at dinner one evening, "why don't you take interim jobs? You're fit now to work in stores or restaurants – even offices, some of you. That way, you'll be earning money and improving your social skills at the same time."

The girls grumbled at first, but did as Vivian suggested. They soon found themselves with regular incomes, working at respectable jobs, planning for advancement, and even going back to school. Their social life involved young men interested in them, not their professional services, and Vivian enjoyed helping the girls give dinner and dancing parties in her home. One by one, the girls moved on, seeking independent lives, but keeping in touch with Vivian and each other. As each girl left, she was replaced by another. The process continued.

Thus it was that what started out to become a high-classed brothel turned into a halfway house for destitute girls, basically financed by the housekeeping allowance awarded Vivian by the divorce court. The two prongs of her original objective had met slightly different targets than those for which she'd aimed, but sometimes that's for the best.

MADAME LIPPINSKI'S FIRST RECITAL
Based on: Burden, Recital, Vague, Coerce

The burden of trying to coerce ten four-year-old ballet students into a vague semblance of a recital was a challenge that Madame Lippinski had never expected to face, but her livelihood depended on her success. With her own dancing career ended by a knee injury and her husband dying of cancer, she had rented this studio in a suburban professional center and hung out her shingle. Response had been encouraging. She had formed four classes, according to age, but this one was the largest, the most lucrative, and her biggest headache.

The ten little girls in black tights and leotards had formed two rows and stood solemnly in first position, waiting for the music and Madame Lippinski's signal to begin. She stood stern-faced before them, her costume like theirs except for a pale blue scarf that formed a filmy skirt over her hips. She raised her arms over her head. Four of the girls followed her, three watched the pianist (one of these with a finger in her nose), three watched themselves in the mirrored wall behind her. She clapped her hands sharply. Twenty eyes came her way. She nodded to the pianist and raised her arms again. Twenty little arms rose in response. She led them into a simple routine to Tchaikovsky's "Waltz of the Flowers." The two rows became a scraggly circle. One girl stopped and raised her hand. The music stopped. "I have to go to the bathroom," said the girl, holding her crotch. Madame Lippinski sighed and nodded. The recital was scheduled for tonight!

Evening came. The hour of seven approached. Two long rows

174

of chairs had been placed along the mirrored wall. Twenty-seven girls arrived in costume, with forty-two parents in tow. Madame Lippinski, dressed in a red satin blouse and long, black, brightly embroidered skirt, greeted them at the door, smiling with a confidence she did not feel, and invited the parents to sit in the chairs. The girls, grouped according to class, sat in front of their parents, on the floor. Madame Lippinski stood in the center of the room and spoke briefly in her heavily accented English. She welcomed the parents, praised the girls for their hard work, and gave an outline of what they had tried to accomplish in this, their first three months. She introduced the four-year-olds, signaled them to their places, took her own place beside the piano.

The music began. The children danced. Not perfectly, but with such charm that their mistakes didn't matter to those who watched them with tears of love blurring their vision.

She introduced the next class, and the next, and next. Each successively older group danced with more precision, more formal grace, and more sophisticated art. Madame Lippinski found her heart going out to each girl as she watched her, remembering her own faltering steps as a young student. She loved them all. This dancing school was no longer a mere matter of livelihood to her. Tonight it had become her life and her joy.

HEART AND SOUL
Based on: Cajole, Anemia, Sonata, Muster

No matter how adroitly Antonio tried to cajole her, Sheila could not overcome the anemia of her enthusiasm for the idea that Beethoven's "Moonlight Sonata," in fusion with a medley of Antonio's own variations on the same theme, could muster an audience for the Spring Concert.

This was not the first time that Sheila had encountered a dilemma of this sort; she had a weakness for young, handsome, aspiring composers. It was not as though she had any romantic hopes for any of these relationships. At an over-ripe and over-plump forty-five, she had all but given up hope in that direction – but not entirely. Dreams die slowly in the passionate heart. Nevertheless, she maintained a stern sense of responsibility for the success of the concerts offered twice a year by the Altonborough Chamber of Commerce. Throughout all of her temptations, she reminded herself that just one failed concert would mean the end of her power; the end of her opportunities for – for what? She was never quite sure what her own ultimate objective was.

Antonio had just left her music room. They had spent the better part of three hours together as he auditioned his music for her on her piano. Afterward, they had sipped sherry and discussed the possibilities of his proposal for a concert. The music had been dull – at times inept – yet his warm dark eyes had held such charm. His long, graceful fingers as they had played over the piano keys and, then, as they held a sherry glass,

176

captivated her. His lilting voice and Latin accents, expounding the visions he had attached to his work, came close to convincing her that it was – as he, himself was – exciting.

Now alone, she went to the piano and, reading the musical scores that he had left with her, replayed it, trying hard to find the excitement in it that would make for a successful concert. At last, she sighed and closed the lid over the piano keys. She gathered up the sheets of music and placed them sadly in their folder. "There's just no hope here," she murmured, but then a thought struck her: This young man has so much life in him; so much grace; so much imagination. Yes, all of that, she thought. Yet in his music, there is something missing.

In an effort to sort out the basic problem, Sheila replayed parts of Antonio's variations, then parts of Beethoven's original text. She sat quietly, then, her eyeglasses dangling from her thumb, her brow furrowed, her eyes lightly closed. "All of art," she heard her father telling her long ago, "is an expression of the soul, and every soul is unique. Imitation is a prostitution of the soul."

"That's it!" she exclaimed to the vacant room. "Antonio not only borrowed Beethoven's theme, he tried to borrow his soul, ignoring his own vibrant spirit."

In the days and weeks that followed, Sheila impressed on Antonio the importance of expressing his own soul throughout his life, and especially through his work. "Always trust your free and naked spirit never to hinder art," she told him again and again. Gradually, the idea permeated his mind and through his mind, his fingers. His music became warm, alive, exciting. The young man who had tempted her heart with his physical grace and beauty now won it with his art; an art that would make a success of the Spring Concert.

Rehearsals began. Publicity ran rampant. People talked. Tickets sold. On the Sunday afternoon of the concert, the performance hall burst with bodies – and then with applause. Antonio was called back onto the stage again and again, beaming and bowing.

At last, on his final appearance, he held up his hands, asking for silence. "There is art in composition of music," he said. "There is art in production of it. Yet, perhaps the greatest art of all is in the encouragement of the free and naked spirit. For that...." and here, he paused and signaled for Sheila to join him on stage, "...for that," he continued, grasping her hand in his, "I ask you to recognize my mentor and your impresario, Sheila McKay."

Once again, the standing audience broke into thunderous applause and Sheila, tears glistening in her eyes, accepted a huge bouquet of red roses, knowing that she had, in aiding in the fruition of this young man's dreams, fulfilled her own.

A NOVEMBER BIRTHDAY
Based on: **Lingered, Bluish, Tardy, Gather**

Agatha lingered in the bluish light of her November garden to gather the tardy-blooming roses and mourn the passing of their season.

It was a lonely time for her. She had begun to think that, like these roses, her time for blooming had long passed; that she was hanging on to life when all around her had died or gone dormant. Today was her seventy-fifth birthday and she was alone. There had been gifts in the mail from both her daughters, cards from a couple of her grandchildren and several friends, and a drawing from a great- grandchild, but there was no one here to hold, to touch, to share a meal with. No one who needed her. No one to comfort her as she felt herself wither like these roses. Wither and fall apart.

It was no one's fault, she reflected. Harry hadn't meant to die. Poor dear, he'd endured his suffering so long that it came as a blessing to see him go. And her dear girls had not chosen to live so far away from her, but there it was. Each person must live his own life, tread his own path.

Agatha shook her shoulders. Enough of that, she told herself.

She followed the line of stepping stones around the side of the house to put those poor dead roses into the trash. No one should have a birthday in November, she thought. It's a time for.... But there I go again. She lifted the lid of the garbage can, dropped the roses inside, and replaced it. "There," she said aloud. "So much for that."

Continuing her circuit of the garden that she and Harry had created all those years ago, and that had fallen to neglect during his illness, she saw much that needed doing. Pruning, weeding, planting of spring bulbs. "It's too much for me to do alone," she thought. "But how pleased Harry would be if I...."

Suddenly, she had a mission. A challenge. A recipient for her love. She had plans to make. Problems to solve. November was not a time to die, but a time to plan for April.

GAMES PEOPLE PLAY
Based on: Taboo, Unlike, Chess, Absurd

"Unlike bridge," said the fizzy blonde to the tall dark geek seated next to her, "chess has some absurd taboo against conversation, so I've never learned to play."

"Thank God for small favors," said the geek.

The blonde wore a frappe of a dress that made her look like a strawberry daiquiri. The geek wore a tux that looked as though it had seen several generations, and he, himself, bore the appearance of a specter from "Hamlet." The blonde knew, though, that this geek was Roger Lanninger, a world-renowned physicist and chess champion. The geek knew that this frivolous-looking blonde was Delia Scott, who headed one of the leading advertising agencies in the country.

Delia and Roger had been seated side by side by their diabolical hostess and, at this point, both were wondering why. Actually, there were two reasons. The first they could have discerned with a little observation of the other eight people at their round table. Delia and Roger were single, whereas all of the others had come in pairs. Her other reason was more convoluted, and calculated in favor of the philanthropic cause they had been invited here to support. They were both wealthy and they were among the most competitive people she knew. If they got into a bidding contest at the auction which was to follow dinner, the numbers could be spectacular.

"Do you play bridge?" asked Delia, ignoring Roger's snide remark.

"Not conversationally," said Roger.

Neither did she, but she wanted to bug him so she asked, "You mean you have to concentrate so completely that you can't engage in a little casual chitchat during play?"

"I simply prefer to do one thing at a time," he told her with a small smirk at the corner of his mouth. "Like eating dinner, for instance."

It takes a lot better looking guy than you to put me in my place, she thought, but she said, "Then I'd better leave you to it or you might eat your napkin and wipe your face with your steak."

He glanced at her out of the corner of his eye and caught the twinkle in hers, but let a few moments of silence intervene while he carved on his steak.

She watched him silently, struck by the exquisite grace of his hands as he handled his utensils, and then tried another gambit.

"Read any good books lately?" she asked.

"*Dynamics of Subterranean Hydraulic Transference,*" he said, keeping his eyes steadfastly on a forkload of food.

"Oh," she said. "No wonder you don't have anything to say over bridge."

"Exactly," he said and filled his mouth sufficiently to excuse his silence for some time, but a length asked, "And you?"

"Oh, books, you mean," she said, pretending to have lost the thread of their conversation. "Well, there are several. Have you read *The Dynamics of Subliminal Communication?*"

That smirk again appeared at the corner of his mouth and it tickled her. It made him look a little like Harrison Ford.

"And did you learn anything?" he asked.

"Quite a bit," she answered. "For instance, it is not possible to communicate with inanimate objects."

"How surprising," he said, and he took another bite, reflecting that there were no inanimate objects involved here.

Suddenly he turned to her and looked directly into her eyes, searching for something clever to say. "How about dinner sometime," he blurted.

"We just tried that," she said, holding his gaze.

"Well then, how about … something physical," he suggested, reddening and feeling like an idiot.

"Is that because you're a physicist?" she asked with a smile in her eyes.

"It's because you're driving me crazy," he confessed.

"How about bowling," she breathed in a sultry voice, mocking him.

"You bowl?" he asked, imitating her suggestive tone.

"I average 265," she lied.

"Shall we leave now?" he asked.

"Now," she said, and they did.

*

Printed in the United States
1223400005B/172-219

9 781592 864263